D0501756

THE WAITING TREE

LINDSAY MOYNIHAN

AMAZON CHILDREN'S PUBLISHING

The characters and events portrayed in this book are fictitious. Any similarity to real persons, living or dead, is coincidental and not intended by the author.

Text copyright © 2013 by Lindsay Moynihan

All rights reserved

No part of this publication may be reproduced, stored in a retrieval system, or transmitted, in any form or by any means, electronic, mechanical, photocopying, recording, or otherwise, without the prior permission of the copyright owner. Request for permission should be addressed to:

Amazon Publishing
Attn: Amazon Children's Publishing
P.O. Box 400818
Las Vegas, NV 89140
www.amazon.com/amazonchildrenspublishing

Library of Congress Cataloging-in-Publication Data available upon request.

ISBN-13: 9781477816349 (hardcover)
ISBN-10: 1477816348 (hardcover)
ISBN-13: 9781477866344 (ebook)
ISBN-10: 1477866345 (ebook)

Book design by Katrina Damkoehler and Susan Gerber
Editor: Margery Cuyler

Printed in The United States of America (R)
First edition
10 9 8 7 6 5 4 3 2 1

PREFACE

Stephen's iPod was set on a loop, blasting Bon Jovi's *Slippery When Wet* at high volume for the tenth time. If it hadn't been for that, I might have heard the rusty hinges of the clubhouse door opening.

Stephen, panting and moaning my name—*Simon*—held tightly to a clump of my hair. He was almost there, I thought, but then I felt his entire body seize.

"Dad!" he screamed. I fell backward in shock and landed hard on my wrists. Stephen clambered onto the bench, a scrap of wood nailed to the wall, and covered himself with his shirt. His jeans were on the other side of the clubhouse, where his father was now standing. I propelled myself off the ground and pulled on my T-shirt as I stumbled to my feet.

Oh my God, I repeated over and over in my head like the looping album on his iPod. Panic rolled inside my stomach and up into my chest. *How did he find us here? He thought we'd grown out of our clubhouse years ago.*

I couldn't look at his dad; I was too afraid. With my arms clamped around my chest, I looked at Stephen in desperation. I'm not exactly sure what I expected him to do. Protect me the way he always did, I guess. Fix this mess because every mess I ever got into was his idea, but he always knew a way out.

Not this time. Stephen had a look of terror in his eyes that I'd never seen in the seventeen years we'd been best friends.

"Sweet Jesus," said a strange voice. It didn't sound like his father, who I loved more than my own. It sounded like an evil space alien, someone who picked up Stephen's jeans and sent them flying to his head. "Get dressed."

Stephen obeyed, and I watched him struggle with his belt buckle and shoes. He stood facing me, his clothes and hair all messed up, and he was crying. His dad towered over him, glaring at me as if his eyes were lasers that could shoot me down right where I stood. I looked back at Stephen, realizing that I might not get another chance to tell him what I'd been trying to tell him all night. "I love you," I said, but I'm not sure he heard me over the sounds of his own sobbing and "Livin' on a Prayer."

His dad grabbed his arm and pulled him toward the door. "You're never seeing this pervert again, you hear me?" said the alien voice. "Y'all are through!"

As the door slammed shut with Stephen on the other side, my whole body started shaking. My knees gave out and I landed on the bench, my head between my legs as I tried to remember how to breathe. Everyone would find out about my secret now: my brothers, my church, *everyone*. But that wasn't why I was afraid to open my eyes, afraid to keep living. Stephen was gone and I didn't know if I was ever going to see him again.

CHAPTER 1

When I was seventeen, I dropped out of high school and took a night job at Pharis's Stop 'n Save. It was summer, and I had to walk in one-hundred degree heat to work, where I'd stay until midnight behind a cash register making seven dollars and twenty-five cents an hour. During the day, I had to look after my twin brother Jude. That's why I worked nights. After my parents died in the car accident, I was all Jude had. *Poor kid.*

I started sweating as soon as I left the house. The store wasn't far, maybe a quarter mile, but it felt like ten miles in that heat. The Stop 'n Save was the only place left in town to buy anything. It was in a strip mall on the east side of town, next to a burger joint, a liquor store, and a greasy diner where my parents used to take us after church.

The strip mall was the unofficial border between the good and bad sides of town. You wouldn't think that with a population of four thousand, Waynesboro, Louisiana, would be large enough to have a "bad side." It somehow managed. I think I would have preferred it if our nice little town had been ruined by heavy industry. At least then there would be jobs. Instead, Waynesboro was dying of neglect, and the desertion in the air reeked more than any factory fumes.

I was almost to the edge of the Stop 'n Save parking lot when I felt the handle bar of a bike slam against my arm. It was too late to make a break to the other side of the street. Stan Rafferty was in front of me, with his skull-and-crossbones-painted mountain bike turned sideways so it blocked the entire sidewalk. To make matters worse, he opened his mouth.

"Hey, faggot," he said. "Where's your boyfriend?"

Stan, three inches taller than I was and seventy pounds heavier, had been the captain of the wrestling team at our high school. Despite having a lower IQ than Waynesboro High's mascot, Slugger the Sea Lion, he graduated with the rest of my old class last month. A lot of good that did him. He worked at the gas station, but I'd heard he was dealing dope on the side.

"Listen, Stani-poo," I said, using the nickname I'd heard his mother call him. "I've got work in ten minutes, and my boss isn't going to believe me if I tell her I was stalked by an abnormally large turd."

He flashed me a crooked grin. I wasn't sure if he was angry or impressed. Since there was nothing to stop him from pounding my face into the pavement if he was angry, I took a few steps back.

"Easy, Peters," he jeered. "I'm not gonna kick your fairy ass, at least not today. But you know what I *am* gonna do? I'm gonna give you some good advice. Put that little retarded brother of yers in a home and get the Hell outta town." He paused for a breath. "And don't ever call me

Stani-poo again or I will make you wish you'd never been born. If you don't wish that already."

Before I had a chance to duck out of the way, a wad of spit smacked my cheek. Stan cackled like it was the funniest thing he had ever seen. I shook my head to get his slobber off before I got infected. Who knew what diseases Stan Rafferty carried?

He stood up on his bike and leaned forward, making it hop off the sidewalk. He peddled away and shouted loud enough for the whole street to hear: "Have fun with your boyfriend, pansy ass!"

An old woman shuffling down her driveway gave me a dirty look. Without even thinking I shouted, "What are you looking at?" She scurried away. Hardly the way my mom raised me to talk to seniors, but whenever anyone brought up Stephen, I just lost it.

Before my family moved to the Stop 'n Save side of town, Stephen and I were next-door neighbors. Together we built a clubhouse out of scrap wood in the ravine behind our houses. That's where Mr. Lévesque caught me going down on Stephen last July. When you're in the middle of doing that, it's real easy to lose track of time. It was past Stephen's curfew, and his dad got a lot more than he bargained for when he went looking for him that night.

The first thing he did was call my brothers to tell them I was a sick perv. Paul and Luke begged the Lévesques to keep it quiet, but there was no chance of that in a town as small as Waynesboro. Stephen's parents felt the need to share the incident with our entire congregation and asked them to pray for us. The minister suggested that the Lévesques ship Stephen off to the Waverley Christian

Center where the healing power of prayer—and maybe a little electroshock therapy—would convince him to leave his gay ways behind.

Within three days, every man, woman, and child at the Cross of Calvary Evangelical Church knew what had happened between Stephen and me. I became the shame of the entire congregation, and it didn't take long for news to spread around town.

I'd thought Paul, my oldest brother, would be on my side. I mean, I never asked to be this way. My life would have been a whole lot easier if I just liked girls. But after the Lévesques called Paul that night, all he could say to me was, "I'm just glad that Mom and Dad aren't around to see how you've turned out." My second brother, Luke, was afraid to argue with Paul. He was the handsome, carefree brother who'd rather joke around than fight. He would flash me a sympathetic look whenever Paul got angry about what had happened, but Luke never stepped up to defend me. They both weren't much for change so they kept going to church every Sunday with Jude like nothing had happened. I kept my distance and I think they—and everyone at Cross of Calvary—preferred it that way.

Losing Stephen made being stuck in Waynesboro even more of a nightmare. There was nobody I could talk to, much less fool around with. It was just me and my hard-on. But more than that, it felt like someone had ripped me into two pieces and hid the other half. I didn't know how to be me without Stephen. I'd never had to try.

I reached the store only five minutes late, but to my managers, Renee and Jeb, that would be five minutes *too* late, so I started to run. I passed through the automatic doors and almost bowled over an old lady who was barely tall enough to see over her shopping cart.

Every time I walked through those doors, I felt like I was being swallowed by this giant monster of consumerism. The place was a warehouse with concrete floors and ceilings so tall I wondered how the lights could shine this far down. The first thing I saw was the row of over twenty cashier stands. With the flashing lights and the constant dinging of the scanners, the place was like a casino, so some of us cashiers started calling it "The Strip" after Las Vegas. On the left was the grocery section, which had a butcher shop, a bake shop, and a fish counter you could practically smell from the sidewalk.

In the middle of every Pharis's Stop 'n Save were rows and rows of cheap clothing, probably made in some Asian sweatshop. Behind the clothes were the toys, jewelry, and electronics. Home goods, tools, and the greenhouse took up the entire right-hand side of the store. Customers could buy anything here: dinner, an engagement ring, and a .28 caliber Colt revolver all in one visit. I hated knowing that a good chunk of my paycheck went back into this place for groceries and clothes and for stupid stuff like the toilet plunger I had to buy last week.

I jogged to the back of the store where the locker rooms were located. The guys' locker room was more of a storage unit with a couch shoved in one corner, a microwave on top of a pile of boxes, and a shopping cart filled with old store flyers. Employee turnover was insanely high so management didn't bother making the place cozy. I'd somehow managed to stick around for an entire year. With Jude to support, I didn't have much of a choice. Most nights there was a newbie sitting in the lounge filling out paperwork and watching the safety video that reminds you to lift heavy stuff from your knees. I peeled off my sweaty shirt and grabbed a clean polo from my locker. Over that I pulled the yellow vest with my nametag and a huge round pin that read *Pharis Sees Your Needs*.

I grabbed my time card and slammed my locker shut. When I walked out of the locker room, Renee was standing in front of the bulletin board looking at next week's schedule. I tried to creep over to the time card machine without her noticing.

"You're ten minutes late, Simon," she said, without even looking up. No way I could sneak anything past a manager equipped with mom-dar. Renee had two little girls at home and had developed this sixth sense for knowing where we all were at any given time.

I swiped my card and put it in my jeans pocket. "Yeah, sorry, Renee. I ran into that Rafferty kid again."

She looked at me sympathetically, and I knew that I was in the clear. "You pay him no mind, Simon. He's a no-good thug." She smiled, revealing a large gap between her middle teeth. "Jump on register seven. You're taking the express lane tonight."

"Yes, ma'am," I replied.

"Oh, and don't forget about my offer," she said. "You're welcome at Christland Baptist anytime. I don't care what them Cross of Calvary fools say about you."

I nodded my head, but any conversation about church made my skin itch, so I wasted no time getting to my register. I did have to duck behind a pantyhose display for a second so as to not be seen by Jeb. Even though he was a regular at our church, Jeb was a lot more like Stan Rafferty than Renee. I knew the sort of guy Jeb was on my first day. After setting me up at my register, he whispered "homo" under his breath and walked away.

I signed onto the machine and flipped the light switch. The express lanes weren't so bad. Customers could only have ten items or less so the line moved pretty quickly. The faster the customers went through, the less time they had to creep me out or to complain about the fact that we had run out of the two-for-one hot dog buns.

At register eight, Tobey Hale was zooming through an order. "Hey, Simon," he said. "How are ya?"

"Fine, thanks," I answered. "When are you off tonight?" It was kind of sad that all conversations started the same way: How are you and when do you get to leave?

"I'm done the same time as you," he said. "I just got here on time." Tobey was a Stop 'n Save veteran and the fastest cashier in the store, probably the fastest in town. I envied Tobey. He actually liked this job.

In the late afternoons the store was a wasteland. Except on Fridays. That was when everybody got their welfare checks. Tobey was bent over his counter, reading an Iron Man comic. I regretted not bringing something to read myself. Even the GED prep book Tobey had given me a few months ago would have been better than just standing around waiting for something to happen.

When the store became quiet, my thoughts drifted and it was like I was back there with Stephen again.

I was running through the streets of Waynesboro in the humid summer air to the ravine behind Stephen's house. Luke had asked where I was going, and in a panic I told him

Stephen and I were getting ice cream. I thought he'd be on to me. After all, I was seventeen, not five. But Luke actually bought into it.

I was getting something tonight, but it wasn't ice cream. Or maybe I was losing something? Technically both. We'd finally decided that it would be tonight, and I had been freaking out all week. I'd almost called Stephen at least six times to tell him that I wasn't ready, but I never did. The reasons were never good enough. Not even my fear of going to Hell. One day, just a month ago, my parents were talking and laughing at the dinner table and the next day they were dead; sandwiched between a semi and the I-10 overpass. I didn't know if they were in Heaven right now or if they were anywhere at all. I didn't know anything anymore, so I decided to just go for it. Carpe frickin' diem.

We had found a new purpose for our abandoned clubhouse at fourteen when we first started making out and didn't want to get caught. We figured no one would ever think to look for us there, so we started sneaking through the neighborhood to the clubhouse a couple of times a week. We never stayed for more than an hour unless we'd told our families we were going to a movie.

I cut through old man Favre's backyard and ran down the hill to the ravine. I came to a stop just outside the clubhouse. My skin itched from adrenaline. Taking a deep breath, I opened the door. Stephen was already inside. He was lighting a row of candles on the coffee table we'd brought from Stephen's house when his mom redecorated. The wooden slab we used as a bench to sit on was covered with a thick blanket and some pillows I recognized from his TV room couch.

"What took you so long?" he asked. "I was starting to think you'd bailed on me."

"Nah," I said. "You know I'm always late. What's all this?"

Stephen shrugged and cracked a mischievous grin. "I figured if I was going to deflower you, I should at least try to make the place look half decent."

"Deflower me?" I laughed. "Is that what they're calling it these days?"

Stephen started laughing too and tossed the lighter he was holding onto the table. "Who the Hell knows," he said. "It just sounded . . . I dunno, romantic." He came toward me with this intense look on his face and gave me a little push against the door. He held my chin and started kissing me ferociously, his tongue moving deep inside my mouth. We had never kissed like this before. The blood began rushing through my body, and I felt that if I didn't have him right that very second, I was going to explode. I pulled up his shirt, grabbing the skin around his waist, and pushed him further back into the clubhouse. We fell onto the bench with a—

BANG!

The crash of the twenty-four-case of water bottles hitting the belt jolted me out of my stupor. "Jesus," I said, trying to catch my breath from the sudden shock.

"Sorry, kid. Didn't mean to scare ya," said the man.

"That's okay." I reached for the scanner gun. "How many of these have you got?"

"Five," he said. "So, having a little daydream, huh?"

"Something like that," I mumbled.

I handed the water man his receipt and peered down

my lane to see a huge line. I looked up at the clock, but I already knew it was around eight-thirty. We always got a rush around eight-thirty, like a busload of people had been dropped off at the store at exactly the same time. At nine, I switched off the light at my register so that no more customers would enter my line. It was break time and my growling stomach and aching feet were ready.

CHAPTER 2

Over the head of my last customer, I could see Tina's raven hair at register fourteen. Her mother was Choctaw, a tribe whose name, Tina had told me, meant "those who listen and see." She was a few years older than I was and had graduated high school a year behind Luke, who had just turned twenty-one.

I didn't notice girls, but the first time I saw Tina, I couldn't help but stare. Her skin was like milky coffee and she had these giant doe eyes. There was something else that drew me to her. Something that reminded me of my mother and of Stephen all at the same time. It was before I started working at the Stop 'n Save. I was checking out at Tina's register with Jude.

"Did you find everything you needed?" she asked as we unloaded our eggs and potatoes. Jude nodded, his eyes glued to her.

"I'm Tina," she said. "What's your name?"

Jude began to sign the letters in his name. Mom had taught him to sign when we were six because he refused to talk. Luke and I had picked up enough to have a conversation with him but Paul, like our dad, refused to make much of an effort. Both of them thought Jude just wanted attention.

"It's nice to meet you," Tina signed back.

My jaw nearly dropped to the ground. Nobody knew sign language in our town.

"And what's your name?" she asked me. I felt like someone had just clicked the off switch on my vocal cords, but I managed to choke out an answer.

"Simon," I said. "I'm his brother. How come you know how to sign?"

"My brother was deaf," she said, and then she looked puzzled. "But Jude isn't deaf, is he? He could hear me when I asked him what his name was."

"No, he's not deaf," I said. "He's mute. That's why he signs."

"Oh," she said, and didn't seem to know what to say next.

"Yeah, it's complicated." I didn't know what to say either. How could I explain Jude? The best doctors around couldn't explain him. When we were growing up, Mom shuffled him across the state to be poked and analyzed. There was nothing wrong with him: he could hear, he could write, he could sign, but he never said a word. He was diagnosed with everything from sensory processing disorder to autism. None of the diagnoses really fit the symptoms. Jude was just Jude. "Maybe your brother can meet Jude sometime," I said. "Not a lot of people around here can sign with him."

Tina's expression changed. "I wish he could," she said, "but Corey died of leukemia three years ago."

Crap, I thought to myself. *Good one, Peters.* I wanted

to tell her I was sorry, but the words just wouldn't come out.

Tina handed me the receipt and turned to Jude, who was standing quietly at the end of the register. His eyes hadn't left her for even a second. She began to talk to him. "You are very special," she said. "There's an old Indian prophecy I was told as a kid. It says from the rising sun there will soon come a different kind of man from any we've ever seen. Maybe that's you?" She winked at Jude, who just stood there smiling.

Tonight Tina was leaning against her register texting furiously. I used to have a decent cell phone before the whole thing with Stephen went down and Paul canceled my number from our plan. We got into a big fight, and he threw my phone into the toilet because he thought I had been "sexting" Stephen. I kind of had been but I wasn't going to tell Paul that. I probably could have saved my phone if Paul hadn't pulled it out of the toilet and smashed it to pieces with his steel-toe work boots. Now all I could afford was one of those cheap pay-as-you-go jobs, which I had to hide from my brothers. Not that it really mattered. I only used it to call Tina. Stephen's cell had been disconnected by the time I got my new phone. His Gmail and Facebook accounts had been closed too.

I walked over to Tina's register. "You hungry?" I asked her.

She peered up from her phone, looking happy to see me. "Starving, but I'm not done with my shift. Just on break. How about you?"

"Yeah, unfortunately, but we have time to go to the Pilot."

The Pilot Café was the diner my parents used to take us to every Sunday. It wasn't far from the municipal airport, and every once in a while planes flew overhead as if to remind me that the people inside them were leaving this crummy town and I wasn't.

Tina slid out from behind her register and took off her banana-colored vest. She threw it carelessly onto the belt. We walked out of the store into the muggy night air.

The Stop 'n Save was lit up like a Christmas tree compared to the darkness of the vacant strip mall. Dining options were pretty limited. It was the Pilot Café or salmonella on a bun at the Burger Shack. It seemed kind of ironic to me: I never wanted to go to the Pilot as a kid and now I was eating dinner there most nights.

I walked along the sidewalk a few paces behind Tina. I could see her spider tattoo crawling beneath her low rider jeans each time she took a step. At this time of night the restaurant was practically empty, except for a line cook and a bored waitress. As always, there was Baptiste, the owner, whose massive body spilled over his stool behind the counter as he did a crossword puzzle. We stood there for a little while, scared to interrupt him. Finally, he looked up with a blank expression on his face. Without saying anything, he handed us menus and nodded his head in the direction of the empty dining room.

The waitress was at our table in less than a minute, excited that she was finally going to get a tip. We both ordered our usual: coffee and grilled cheese sandwiches. As soon as the waitress left, Tina flopped back in her seat, revealing the rose tattoo just above her hip bone. She let out a dramatic sigh.

"Now what's wrong?" I asked.

"Men," she huffed. "What else?"

"Let me guess, dream boy Dillon's not working out?"

"He's gone," she replied. "I dumped his sorry ass."

"Good," I said. "He was a waste of time, just like all the others."

For a pretty girl, Tina had a pretty low opinion of herself. She dated one loser after another. Dillon was the latest guy, and it was obvious to everyone but her that he just wanted to get inside her pants. Tina was afraid of going for five minutes without a boyfriend so she settled for the trash she could pick up in the trailer park where she lived with her sister and her grandmother.

"You need to stop dating those pricks from your neighborhood," I said, as I poured tons of sugar into my sludgy coffee. "We've talked about this a thousand times."

"So where am I going to meet men?" she whined. "At the Cross of Calvary Evangelical Church where a girl can't even kiss a guy before she's married? At least Dillon knew how to have fun!"

"You mean Dillon knew how to get you into bed? Believe me, that's not the same thing as fun."

Tina let out a dramatic huff. "Well, you're a guy, so I guess you would know," she said.

"Maybe one of these days you'll actually listen to me."

Tina needed to meet a guy who was the straight version of Stephen. Someone who was looking for a deeper connection than the kind you get from a hookup. Stephen and I were happy just to be with one another, even if we weren't doing anything at all. He was all gung ho about sex way before I was ready. Frankly, I was afraid if I started blowing him I would start lisping and walking with a swagger like the gay guys on TV. But Stephen loved me enough to wait. When it finally did happen, I was relieved to discover that I was the same kind of guy I'd always been.

Tina flashed me one of her mischievous smiles. "Too bad I couldn't find someone like you," she said. "I can talk to you about anything."

I raised an eyebrow. Tina seemed to think my gayness was a phase. She was under the impression I could be converted with a little flirting or girly eye batting. "Don't you think a boyfriend like me would kind of defeat the purpose?" I asked.

Tina started laughing, and out of the corner of my eye, I could see Baptiste watching us.

"Maybe," she said, lowering her voice to a whisper. "But seeing as how we're shopping in the same market, you can help me pick out a good one this time."

"Well, I can at least tell you which ones to avoid," I said. "And don't bother whispering, I'm pretty sure the entire state knows by now."

I pulled out five bucks and tossed it onto the table. Our bill was always the same. Tina had stopped laughing and was looking at me seriously.

"So how's Stephen doing?" she asked.

I shrugged, not really knowing what to say. "Fine, I guess. He doesn't tell me much. I've gotten four letters from him, but he doesn't go into detail about the place."

"Huh, that's weird," said Tina. "Why not?"

"Dunno. They're like what you'd write in a postcard. You know, 'Weather's nice. Miss you lots. Blah blah blah.'"

"Have you asked him to tell you more about it?" she asked.

"No, I've never written back. I'm afraid they're reading his mail."

Tina raised an eyebrow, which she always does when she disagrees with something you've said. "Isn't that like against your first amendment rights or something?" she said. "He's probably afraid to tell you about the place because he thinks you'll worry."

"Maybe," I said. I took a deep breath and decided to tell her something that had been bothering me for weeks, maybe even months. "You know what I'm really worried about? I'm worried about it *not* being bad. I mean, what if it's this really nice place and they do change him? When he gets out, he might never want to see me again." I rubbed my eyes and face hard like I could scrape away the nagging thoughts that never left my mind, even when I was sleeping.

"Come on. You don't actually believe that?" Tina chided.

"Why not?" I shot back. "How am I supposed to know? He won't tell me anything, and it's not like I can go see him."

"Oh, bull," she said. "The only reason you can't see him is because they say you can't, and when have you ever given a crap about what they say?"

I wanted to agree with her, but the truth was that I used to care a lot about what my brothers and the people at our church said.

"I think you should go see him," she continued. "I mean, really, what have you got to lose?"

Tina was giving me one of those "I'm not giving up on this one" looks, so I decided to make a bargain with her. "Fine," I said. "I'll figure out some miracle way to see Stephen if you promise to go on at *least* three dates with the next guy before you jump into the sack with him."

"Deal," she replied smugly, thinking she'd won the argument. That seemed to make her happy, and she finished her sandwich with a satisfied little smile on her face. She added another five dollars to the table, and we got up to leave. Tina raced past Baptiste, but as I walked by I smiled and said, "Thanks a lot."

He nodded and it looked as if he were trying to smile, but just couldn't remember how. "See you, kid," he said and then went right back to his puzzle.

"Did he talk to you?" asked Tina when we got outside.

"Well, sort of."

"Wow, he must like you."

I shrugged. "Baptiste doesn't like anybody."

We walked slowly back to the store because we still had seven minutes left in our break. Tina held my arm as we walked. I kept thinking about our deal. I doubted she could hold up her end without me watching her like a hawk. She was way too impulsive, and the drinking didn't help. But if she slipped, would I use that as an excuse to not visit Stephen? Guess I needed her even more than she needed me.

We stood in front of the neon Stop 'n Save sign. It was late, and the pimply teenager who greeted everyone with a phony smile and a "Welcome to Pharis's Stop 'n Save" had gone home for the night. Without saying a word to each other, we walked through the automatic doors.

"Don't forget your end of the bargain," she said, as she turned in the direction of her register.

"I won't if you keep up yours," I challenged.

"Consider it done. Hey, do you want a ride home?" she asked.

"You know it," I said gratefully. "Thanks."

"No worries. See you at twelve."

I walked down the line of beeping machines and flashing lights to register seven. I turned on my light, entered my pass code, and prepared myself for two and a half hours of waiting. Five minutes later, Monique Perry, the loudest cashier of all, came scurrying up to my register.

"Simoooon!" she cooed. "Guess what, hon? I found a real cute thing who was hiding in Home Goods, but I found her and she's definitely single."

"Listen, Monique," I said. "I really appreciate all your hard work and stuff, but I've got it covered. I'm fine. Really."

"Got it covered! Nuh-uh. If you've got it covered, then what's her name?"

I had to think fast. "You can't say anything, all right?"

She started giggling and covered her mouth with her hands. Her nails were bright pink today. "I swear I won't say a thing."

I came in closer and whispered into her ear. "It's Tina."

Monique gasped and then sort of shrieked. I jumped back and hit my elbow on the coupon dispensing machine.

"Ooooh, living on the wild side! Well, your secret's safe with me. But as your social consultant, I want all of the details. You hear me? All of them."

"You bet, Monique," I said. A kid about my age came

up to my register with school supplies. I was never so grateful to see a customer. "Well, I gotta go."

"Okay, hon, I'm off anyways. But I'll be talking to you soon." She winked at me and strutted away.

Great, I thought. I was now at the center of a Stop 'n Save soap opera. I'd have to warn Tina, but at least she'd find it funny.

I wasn't very busy for the rest of the night. Tobey and I talked when we didn't have any customers. He showed me his ring again. The one he got from winning the Chubbe Burger hamburger eating contest.

When midnight came and the store closed, a wave of excitement flooded the place. We ran to the locker rooms, changed, clocked out, and then left the store, relieved to have survived another day.

I met Tina outside the women's locker room, and we walked to her rusting Sunfire. I told her that Monique now thought we were dating.

"Don't worry." She chuckled. "I'll play along."

"I don't want any games," I said. "I just want Monique to quit trying to set me up."

"I know," she said. "But chill a little. There *are* worse things."

I nodded. She was right. We climbed into her car and cranked down the windows so we'd get a little breeze. Her AC had been broken since last summer. The drive wasn't long and in a few minutes, Tina's car puttered to a stop in front of my house. It looked less worn down in the dark, but no more inviting. I thanked Tina for the ride.

"Are you going back to your place?" I asked.

"Not if I can help it," she replied. "I think I'll go to The Toucan."

The Toucan was a dive bar on the outskirts of town where the bartenders didn't care if you were one hundred, twenty-one, or twelve—as long as you could pay. Tina told me that the owner made his own moonshine at his house in the middle of the woods.

"So, when are you gonna take me to this infamous Toucan?" I asked.

"You free Sunday night?"

"Hmm, let me see," I said, pretending to be thinking. "Yeah, I have a feeling my calendar is pretty open." This made Tina laugh. "Well, take it easy," I said.

"You too," she replied. "I'll come by around seven on Sunday."

I waved to Tina as she drove down the street, her car rumbling and wheezing like it didn't want to go home either.

CHAPTER 3

Number twelve was dark inside except for the flickering light of the TV that I could see through the window. I walked into the hall where all of our sweatshirts hung on top of one another and our shoes lay in piles.

Jude and Luke were watching TV in the living room. The fluorescent light poured from the screen and danced against the dark walls. I stared at the source of the light in a trance. I didn't even know what I was watching.

"Hey, little brother," said Luke. "How was work?" He yawned loudly and stretched his long arms over his head. Jude, who was sitting up perfectly straight on the couch, turned and smiled. We didn't look at all like twins. Jude was three inches shorter than me and a lot scrawnier, but everyone—especially our mother—said we had the same smile, especially our mother.

"It was good," I lied. "Not too many jerky customers, and I had dinner with Tina. She gave me a ride home."

"Nice," replied Luke. "I gotta meet y'all at the Pilot sometime. I haven't hung out with Tina since high school. She really filled out senior year." Luke winked at me and then turned his attention back to the TV.

"Just let me know," I said. "We're there most nights. So, how was your day?" I asked him.

"Oh, the same old. Cars come in broken and leave fixed."

Luke had wanted to be a doctor. When I was six, he said he'd pay me a week's allowance to break my arm so that he could fix it. That plan ended when Dad caught me slamming my arm against the weed whacker because falling out of a tree hadn't worked. Luke had been accepted to universities just weeks before the car crash, but after the funeral I found the school brochures in the garbage. He became a mechanic at Emmaus's Garage, which seemed to suit him. I guess if he couldn't fix people, he could at least fix cars. The truth was, Luke could fix just about anything. He was the glue that held our family together and without him we'd have probably killed each other ages ago.

I walked over to where Jude sat on the couch. "Did you have a good night?" I asked him.

Jude shook his head. "Paul got angry," he signed, and then he hung his head and started wringing his hands.

"Did Paul yell at him again?" I asked Luke. *Jesus*, I thought. I was home less than five minutes, and I was already pissed off.

Luke looked up from his show and patted Jude on the back. "Don't worry, Simon," he said, "Paul's stressed is all. I stopped him before he could do any real damage." He leaned in closer to Jude. "Ain't that right, little buddy? No harm done." Luke held Jude's hands so he'd calm down. "Easy, pal," he said. "You need these things to talk to us, so don't be pulling 'em apart." Jude smiled and leaned his head against Luke's shoulder.

"So what happened?" I asked.

"It was nothing, stupid stuff. Jude here accidentally broke a plate."

"Paul freaked out over a plate?"

"Yeah, I told you his head is screwed on too tight. He was all jittery when he got home from work, and the crash of the plate hitting the floor set him off."

"Where's he now?"

"Asleep."

"When did Lydia leave?"

"I dunno, an hour ago tops."

"Christ," I said with disgust. "Why does she even bother going home? We all know what they do up there."

"Watch your mouth," Luke scolded.

I wanted to call him a big fat lying hypocrite, call *both* him and Paul that, but I never had the guts to fight with Luke. I was too afraid he'd get sick of it all and leave.

"Sorry," I said. I looked at Jude falling asleep on Luke's shoulder. "I think it's time for bed."

"Good plan," said Luke. "Do you want me to take care of him? You look beat, little bro."

"Nah," I said, "I got it."

Luke nodded and turned to Jude. "Okay, good night, little buddy." He kissed him on the head and started flipping through the channels. I followed Jude up the stairs to our room, shaking my fist at Paul's bedroom door as we passed.

Paul slept in our parents' old room, which meant he thought he was the man in charge. Not that I envied him. I could hear him pacing at night, slouching under the burden of responsibility that never should have been his. He loved us too much to leave, but not enough to hide his contempt for the cage that the accident put him in. I would have felt sorry for Paul if it wasn't for his she-devil girlfriend, Lydia, who tried to boss me around like she was my stand-in mother. My brothers and I nicknamed Paul "the Captain" when our parents died and he started running the house like an army boot camp.

Jude followed me into our cramped bedroom. He still needed my help to get ready for bed. As for most things, Jude had a bedtime ritual. He'd start with his socks and then move upwards, finishing with his shirt. As he removed one article of clothing, he'd put on the corresponding part of his pajamas. Then he'd go to the bathroom and brush his teeth for exactly three minutes, and then he'd floss for one minute and comb his hair for thirty seconds, counting backward in his head: Thirty Mississippi, twenty-nine Mississippi, twenty-eight Mississippi . . .

He'd kneel down at his bed perfectly straight and pray. He seemed to have this aura about him, like a bubble of glowing light. I always wanted to know what he prayed for, but I never took the time to ask him. Our pastor at Cross of Calvary once said during a sermon that God owes us nothing because we are sinners.

Stephen groaned when he heard this. "If nobody ever made a mistake, then we wouldn't even need a God," he whispered in my ear.

At that time I just brushed off what Stephen said, deciding to toe the Pastor Ted line a little longer. It was so much easier not questioning everything anyways.

CHAPTER 4

"I can't do this," I said. "My dad's a Neanderthal, he'll never understand."

Stephen sat down next to me on the couch. Jude was engrossed in a word search on the old brown recliner. I'd been thinking about coming clean to my parents for a while. The knowledge of what I was had been weighing on my mind to the point I couldn't sleep anymore. Not saying anything just made it worse, turning my whole life, and Stephen, into a dirty secret.

"I think he'll understand more than my dad will," Stephen replied.

"More than your dad isn't much to work with, Stephen," I pointed out. "He's an ex-Marine."

Stephen nodded. "And on the board of our church."

"That too."

"You know, maybe it's none of their business," he said.

"How do you figure?"

"I just mean that parents boss around their kids, but adults can live their lives however they want to. Maybe we just hang tight 'til we're eighteen."

"So what do we do until then?" I asked.

Stephen flashed me a crooked grin. "Run away and join the circus? Maybe they could use a couple of extra freaks."

My eyes opened to the sound of Jude opening and closing drawers. My brothers woke up at seven, if not earlier, to go to work. Once Jude heard a single foot hit the creaky stairs, he was out of bed and starting his morning routine. Afterward, he'd come back into our room and turn the light on. By then, I was half awake and trying to fight off the evil light with my pillow. I was always tired, as if I hadn't slept at all. Sometimes, I felt terrified to get up and start another day all over again. After a couple of minutes of near suffocation, I'd give up and throw the pillow that was over my head onto the floor. Jude would be carefully making his bed and after I'd made mine, he'd straighten it up so that it was as neat as his own.

Jude's side of the room was as organized as a science lab. My side was a different story. I never had time to organize my own stuff so it just sort of mounded up over time, but I always knew where to find things. A pile of books lined my bed. Most of them were my mom's, which she had collected over the years to understand Jude's condition better. I stopped reading those a while ago because all of the best treatments and schools cost so much money, and it was frustrating that we couldn't afford any of them.

When Jude was little he was labeled mentally retarded, but our mother knew better. Dad was ready to put him in some daycare where he would flap his hands all day, but our mom finally stood up to Dad and insisted Jude be homeschooled. Jude proved all the doctors wrong. Our mother was obsessed with teaching Jude anything and everything that he could absorb, no matter how much he protested.

"We have to show him everything," Mom always said. "Show him how to learn, show him how to *try* to learn."

After the accident, I kept up with his lessons as best I could. Despite the obstacles, I think Mom and I did well by Jude. He could dress and feed himself, he could read, and he was getting a lot better about not making a scene when he was tired or scared. But he still couldn't speak. When I was younger, I asked Jude why he didn't talk, and he signed to me that he just couldn't. When I got older, I asked him why he *couldn't* talk.

"I can," he signed. "I let my hands do the talking."

"But don't you want a voice?" I asked him.

"I do have a voice."

"But you communicate in a different language," I reminded him. "So there's a lot of people out there who don't understand your voice." I remember he looked so sure of himself.

"They will," he signed. "Right now, they're just not listening."

I rolled out of bed and pulled on some clothes, probably the same clothes I wore yesterday. Jude was waiting for me by the door. If I was up, he always waited for me before he went downstairs. He'd learned the hard way not to go near Paul without backup.

This particular morning, Paul was sitting at the kitchen table drinking coffee and Luke was leaning against the sink inhaling a bowl of cereal. He'd eat at least two more bowls before he left for the shop. Lydia was planted in a seat next to Paul. If she had an opening shift at the clothing store where she worked, she'd sometimes honor us with her presence at breakfast. I just wanted them all to hurry up and leave so I could call the Waverley Christian Center again. I had tried once, but I'd chickened out and hung up on the lady as soon as she answered the phone. The letters Stephen had sent were total bullshit, which was why I worried about what that place might have done to him. I had to find a way to talk to him, especially now that I'd made that promise to Tina. There was no way I could just show up at the Center unannounced asking to see him.

Paul was staring out the window, looking agitated. I walked into the kitchen and went straight to the coffeepot.

"Good morning, sunshine," Lydia said to Jude in her overly sweet voice, which was as fake as her squirt-bottle blonde hair.

Jude signed "hello," which was the only sign she understood.

"Hey, little buddy. You hungry?" Luke asked Jude.

Jude nodded. I opened the freezer and took out two blueberry Stop 'n Save brand waffles, which is what Jude had been eating for breakfast every single morning since he was seven. I dropped the waffles in the toaster, Jude's cue to get a knife and fork from the drawer and a plate and some Aunt Jemima syrup from the cupboard. He sat down at the table next to Lydia and bobbed back and forth with excitement.

After a couple of minutes of silence, Lydia was itching to talk. "So, what are you guys gonna do today?" she asked me.

"Play in their little garden and try not to break any plates," answered Paul irritably, still looking out the window. Luke swallowed hard on a mouthful of cereal and started coughing.

"It was just a stupid plate," I shot back. "Why do you have to make such a big deal out of everything?" I pulled Jude's waffles out of the toaster early so that he would focus on eating them and not on us arguing. They were still kind of soggy.

"Hey," interjected Lydia, "cut your brother some slack. He's got a lot on his mind, no thanks to you."

I looked at her in disbelief. "Was I *talking* to you?"

Luke stopped coughing and grabbed my arm. "Leave it, Simon," he said quietly. "It's not worth it."

I pulled my arm away. Sometimes, it made me crazy how calm Luke was. Didn't he see what she was doing to Paul . . . to this family? Lydia was about to give me a piece of her empty mind when Paul stepped in.

"Okay, just cut it out," he said.

"But he—"

"It's all right, Lydia," he continued. "Simon's right, the plate thing was stupid. It had nothing to do with the plate anyways, or Jude, it's work. It's always work." Luke and I gawked at each other in amazement.

I looked at Paul, and he really did seem worn out. His face was older, and he had dark circles under his eyes. I felt guilty and thought maybe I *should* cut him some slack.

I took my coffee and sat down in the rickety chair next to Paul. He was looking at me like a human being and not like a perpetual pain in his ass. He grabbed my shoulder and shook it playfully. He was so much like our dad. A good slap on the back was a sign of affection.

"Hey, kiddo," he said to me. "Don't worry. I'm not mad

at you guys, at least not right now, I'm not." He started laughing, and so Lydia joined in. I could see the age lines around Paul's lips. How many twenty-six-year-olds have age lines?

"So what happened at work?" I asked him. "How's old Perrucci?"

Joseph Perrucci owned the JP & Sons Construction Company where Paul had been working for the last three years.

"Old Perrucci's going senile. He's taking construction jobs that he shouldn't be taking because he needs the money, then yesterday, he turns around and pays these newbie punk kids the same wage as me. He says he wants to test them out because he wants to hire them or something." Paul was shaking his head, getting himself all revved up again, while Lydia rubbed his back.

"Man, that sucks," said Luke as he wolfed down another bowl of cereal, but he didn't look like he really cared.

"Those kids," I asked. "Were they any good?"

Paul's eyebrows furrowed. "What do you mean, were they any good? What difference does it make? It's not right that they got paid the same as me. I've been working my ass off for that man for three years."

"Well, maybe Perrucci was paying them for the amount of work they did, not how long they worked there. Maybe he thought he was being a better boss by treating the new guys the same as his longtimers. You shouldn't take it so personally."

Out of the corner of my eye, I could see Luke holding

his breath, waiting for something to explode. Usually I could see it coming too, but not this time. Paul's face was stony as he rose from his chair as if in slow motion, but before I could react, his hand struck the side of my face. The room fell silent. Nobody said anything. Nobody *ever* said anything. My face stung but I was more ashamed than hurt or angry. I stared at the yellow kitchen wall, wanting it to swirl into a vortex that I could just fall into.

"You okay, Simon?" Luke whispered.

"Yeah," I answered. "Terrific, thanks for asking." I jumped up from my chair and took Jude's syrupy plate. He had his hands on his ears. He hated loud noises.

"Listen, Paul," said Luke, his voice cautious. "I think you need to cut out this temper of yers. You take every-thing we say the wrong way these days."

"No, *you* listen," Paul shouted. "I'm the oldest, and Mom and Dad left *me* in charge. And quite frankly, I think I'm doing the kid a favor." This caught my atten-tion. He was talking about me as if I wasn't even in the room. "Simon had no respect for our parents, he has no respect for me, and I can guarantee you that if they had been harder on him growing up, he wouldn't have ended up like one of *those* people!"

"Oh, right," I shot back. "You're such a goddamn hero!"

Paul threw his hands up in frustration. "You see what I mean?" he said to Luke. "He doesn't give a damn that I'm trying to save him from himself."

"Save me from myself?" I shouted. "I never asked you or anybody else to save me because I don't need saving. This is how I am and how I'm gonna stay, so *you* are going to have to deal with it because you can't just beat it out of me." I was breathless, but was ready to run in case he came after me.

"You're impossible, you know that?" said Paul angrily. "You should be grateful to have someone like me around watching out for you. We could of just shipped you off like Stephen, but *I* kept you." He was almost pleading with me. "You should be *grateful.*"

Paul motioned to Lydia who rose from her seat like she was royalty and followed him out of the kitchen, glaring at me. I couldn't stand it anymore, having my own brother hate me. I felt less than human and I knew that I couldn't let Paul leave like this. I followed him into the hall.

"Wait," I said. "Listen, I *am* grateful, but with you it's like I can't win. So, just tell me what I have to do so that we can live in the same house without killing each other."

Paul eyed me carefully. "Lydia, go wait in the car," he said. She reluctantly obeyed, leaving us alone to talk.

"Okay, Simon," he began. "Here's how it's gonna be. This was Mom and Dad's house, but now it's mine and we're gonna play by *my* rules. You change or you get out. You go back to church, and you *promise* me that there'll be no more fooling around. Do we understand each other?"

Was Paul *blackmailing* me? "B-b-but if you throw me out on the street, who will take care of Jude?" I stammered.

"Come on, Simon," he said, his voice flat but threatening. "Do you think Jude would stay here without you? Not a chance. He'd be out on those streets the second you left and then *you'd* be responsible for making your helpless mute brother homeless. So, with that in mind, do we have a deal?"

I nodded. What else could I do?

"Great," he said, looking real satisfied with himself. "See how easy that was? It'll be nice to have the real you back." He walked quickly out of the house.

The real me? I thought. *What was I now, the fake me? Would I suddenly wake up and discover I'd dreamt up this* *entire year or had been in some sort of coma? Paul didn't consider that the person he wanted me to be—the quiet, obedient me—was the real phony.* I looked over my shoulder. Luke was standing in the door to the kitchen.

"Everything okay, little bro?" he asked.

"Yeah, it's fine," I said. "It's Paul. What can I say? His way or the highway, right?"

Luke nodded. "Well, for what it's worth, I agreed with what you said. Paul totally overreacted with that whole pay thing at work. Jude thinks you're right too."

"Thanks," I said, rubbing my sore face. "But I don't think my jaw agrees all that much."

Luke chuckled. "Here, let the doctor look at that for you." He came closer and pretended to examine my face. "Yup, just as I thought. Looks like I'm gonna have to amputate. Well, it's a good thing you know sign language, kiddo." He chuckled.

A minute ago I wouldn't have thought it possible I could laugh about getting smacked. That was Luke for you.

"Well, I gotta run," he said. "You guys have a good day and stay out of trouble, if that's possible."

"It's possible, just not that probable."

Luke grabbed his sports bag and left the house still chuckling, like he didn't have a care in the world.

CHAPTER 5

After Luke left, I took a few minutes to think things through. I knew I could beat Paul at his own game. He couldn't read my thoughts and as long as I kept my mouth shut, he couldn't do anything. It looked as if my mute twin would have to do the talking for both of us. Jude could say whatever he wanted and even though Paul'd get mad, he would never stoop so low as to hit Jude or kick him out.

Jude popped his head around the kitchen door, and I snapped out of my daze. "Sorry about all the yelling," I said. "Did you like your waffles?"

Jude nodded. "I'm not finished. Is he gone?" he signed.

"Yeah," I said, "but don't be scared of him because he won't do anything to you. You know I wouldn't let him."

"I'm not scared of him," he signed. "I don't want you to be scared either."

"Don't worry, I'm not," I lied. "Listen, why don't you go finish your breakfast? I have something I gotta do real quick."

Jude turned and went back into the kitchen like nothing had happened. I had only about five minutes before he'd finish breakfast, so I ran to the telephone next to the couch in the living room. I had the number to the center memorized. Not like it was difficult—1-800-254-SAVE. Once I had found out the name of the place Stephen had been sent to, it was easy enough getting the telephone number online at the library.

The Lévesques had refused to tell me where they'd sent Stephen, even when I showed up at their house at ten o'clock at night and banged on the door for over an hour. Paul had to come and drag me away. Paul knew where Stephen was, he must have, but he pretended he didn't. After that, I started eavesdropping on people's conversations at church. I got lucky one day when one of Mrs. Lévesque's friends spilled everything to the worship team's pianist when they thought they were alone. The second I had what I needed, I left the Cross of Calvary Church and had no intention of ever going back.

My fingers became slippery with the sweat dripping down my hand as I dialed the numbers on my parents' ancient rotary phone. My heart beat painfully against my chest with each ring. I went over in my head what I'd say. "Hello, this is Todd, the assistant youth pastor at the Cross of Calvary Church. Is Stephen available please?" I figured I wouldn't get very far giving them my real name. After all, if Stephen was in that place for a cure, then I was the disease.

A lady finally answered. "Waverley Christian Center, can I help you?" She sounded even more indifferent than the sixteen-year-old who worked the customer service desk at the Stop 'n Save.

I began to stutter and finally blurted out something. "Ah, I'm ah, I'm Todd, the ah youth pastor, no um pastor's assistant at the Cross of Calvary Church. Is Stephen there?" There was silence on the other end. *Damnit!* I thought. *There's no way she bought that.*

"O-kay," she said slowly. "Um, give me a second. I have to check his file for approved callers. Please hold." The phone clicked and worship music came on. It was a song I knew so I tried to focus on the words and not on the fact there was no assistant youth pastor at our church, let alone one named Todd who happened to be on Stephen's approved call list.

I should have just hung up because a few seconds later the music cut off and a man began shouting in my ear. "We're on to you, don't think we aren't! Calling here with your serpent tongues! Damn atheists!" There was another clicking noise, followed by the dial tone.

"What the Hell was that?" I whispered and dropped the beeping phone onto the cradle. I was just going to have to show up unannounced after all.

I pulled myself up and walked through the hallway to the kitchen. Jude had stacked his breakfast dishes neatly in the sink and was rummaging through the broom cupboard. He came out with a bucket full of his gardening tools and left through the back door. I followed him outside.

Our mother loved flowers, but she wasn't much of a gardener. When she died, we inherited yellowing mats of thick grass and dirt patches. It turned out to be a blessing in disguise since the garden provided the perfect activity for Jude and the perfect distraction for me. I hauled around bags of dirt and plants for him, and he laid out the flower patches. It was rough at first. Paul didn't want to help us pay for the supplies we needed. But even Paul had to admit that I was right this time. It turned out that Jude could make anything grow, even strange things like a fig tree.

The back garden, maybe a hundred square feet, was enclosed by a wood fence stained cherry red. There was much less grass in the garden after we dotted the yard with flowers and puffy green bushes. And then there was the fig tree. Out of nowhere one day, Jude got the idea that a fig tree would complete his garden and after a few months of saving, we had enough money to buy an already five-foot tree from an orchard. I wondered why he wanted the fig tree in the first place. Eventually its canopy would blanket most of the garden, blocking the sun. Its thick roots would rob the soil of all its nutrients, causing the rest of the garden to die. I told him all of this, but he just signed that I worried too much.

A mammoth gray rock stood a few yards from the tree, sheltered by the shade of its leaves. We had no idea how it ended up in the backyard, but it was there when our parents bought the place, and it was too heavy to remove. Jude and I sat by the tree a lot, leaning against the rock, talking or reading. Jude said he could close his eyes in the garden and see his whole family. He planted roses for Tina, lavender for our mother, a droopy peony for Luke that reminded him of the cologne Luke wore, and a planter box of rosemary for me. He said he could smell the herb in the aftershave I used. I didn't even know there was rosemary in my aftershave until I read the bottle. I noticed right away that our dad and Paul didn't have a place in Jude's garden.

Growing up our dad kept his distance from Jude. I think he was scared of his son who wasn't like everyone else's kids. Scared of what it said about him as a father or maybe even him as a person. It wasn't his fault just like it wasn't our mother's fault, although some people thought that she drank during her pregnancy. But I think our dad blamed himself anyways, like he was being punished by God, and I felt sorry for him. I knew what it was like. I often wondered why I was different and if it was my fault. If I could have stopped it or changed it. I wished, like Dad probably did about Jude, that someone out there had the answers.

CHAPTER 6

Jude was kneeling by a flower patch pulling out weeds and tossing them into his gray bucket. It wasn't even ten in the morning, and it was already eighty-five degrees outside. I sat under the shade of the fig tree and leaned against its bumpy trunk. I loved these quiet times. Jude, me, and the garden. The only thing missing was Stephen. He used to love Jude's garden, and unlike me, he knew a thing or two about plants. He got that from his parents. He told me once that he liked the garden because it was where we kissed for the first time. I was thirteen and he'd just turned fourteen. I had known for a while that my feelings for him were changing, but Stephen wasn't acting any differently, so I couldn't tell if he felt the same way I did.

We were in his TV room watching Lethal Weapon *one day after school, and my hand kind of slid over to his knee. I pulled it back in a panic and began stuttering an apology, something about how my hand had gone numb from being the catcher in gym class.*

"Don't worry about it," he said with a laugh. "I don't mind."

I was relieved, but far from feeling at peace with the whole thing. I wanted to do a lot more than just put my hand on his knee and while a part of my brain was saying, "Go for it," another part was screaming, "You'll go to Hell for thinking these things, let alone actually doing them!" Over the next few weeks, this battle went on inside my head, and Stephen must have noticed because he asked if we could hang out in my backyard.

"What are we gonna do out there?" I asked. "It's a bug factory."

"Just trust me," he replied.

He led the way to a particularly overgrown section of the yard and dropped down onto the grass. I sat down next to him. We were completely hidden from view. I began to fidget as the urges began stirring up inside of me again.

"Great, Steve, now what?" I complained. My entire body was itching and it wasn't from the bugs. Next, I felt his hand on my back. It was cool against my sweaty T-shirt. I turned to look at him and his face came right up to mine; then he kissed me. He pulled away just as quickly with a satisfied look on his face.

"See? That wasn't so hard," he said. I tried to say something, but nothing would come out.

"How long have you known . . . ?" He didn't complete the sentence.

"How long have you known?" I blurted right back. I couldn't tell if I was the happiest I'd ever been or if I was in complete shock.

"Probably a lot longer than you have," he said, and then he leaned forward to kiss me again.

• • •

I was almost asleep when a deafening crash exploded behind me. Jude cried out and threw his hands over his ears. I jumped to my feet and stood on the gray rock so I could see over the fence into the Raffertys' yard. I couldn't believe it. Stan was using his father's Remington semi-automatic deer hunting rifle to explode a row of beer bottles. When he was finished, he put the safety on and reached into a box for more bottles.

"Hey!" I shouted. "What the Hell are you doing, Stan? You're gonna get somebody killed!"

"Go to Hell!" Stan shouted back. "You're turning into a woman, Simon, or maybe I should call you *Simone* from now on."

"Cute," I said. "We'll see how tough you are, *Stani-poo*, when you shoot somebody and get a one-way ticket to Angola."

I jumped down from the rock as Stan cursed at me through the fence. I felt a rush of adrenaline. It wasn't very often that I won an argument with Stan Rafferty.

I collapsed onto the grass. The smell of rotting garbage drifted over from the Raffertys' backyard. Their whole house looked like it threw up on our street and now, thanks to Stan, broken bottles and bullet shells were strewn all over the brown grass.

I was about to go escape from the smell when Jude tapped my shoulder.

"It's noon," he signed. "Time for lunch."

Jude was very particular about what and when he ate. "Let's go," he urged me. "Peanut butter and banana today. It's Friday."

"Okay, I'm coming." I pulled myself up from the

ground. My tired body felt heavier than the seventy-two-inch flat screen TV I had to carry to a lady's car the other day at work. We walked back toward the house. Jude took his shoes off on the mat outside the kitchen door. He looked down in disgust at my dirty shoes. I rolled my eyes at him as I stepped out of them.

He smiled, knowing he drove me crazy sometimes. "It's my job as your twin to keep an eye on you," he signed.

I laughed and gave him a little push into the house. "In that case, don't you have more important things to worry about than my shoes?" I joked.

Once inside, I grabbed eight pieces of bread so that we could each have two sandwiches. I bought green bananas every Monday so they'd be ripe by Friday. Everyone in the house knew not to eat those bananas.

Jude placed the sandwiches on two dinner plates, and I got our drinks. We sat at the kitchen table eating our lunch. Jude finished quickly and went to the sink to wash off his plate. I had been chewing on the same piece of sandwich for what felt like forever.

"It's too hot in the garden," Jude signed. "Let's make some cookies for Mrs. Rafferty."

"But Stan is there," I protested. "We can't go now."

"Sure we can," he signed. He pulled a cookie dough package out of the freezer.

"But he's such a jerk!" I yelled.

"Maybe he's a jerk because he doesn't know what it means to be kind," he signed. "We should show him."

"Whatever," I said. "You can do what you want, but I'm not going over there."

Jude smiled and carried on making his damn cookies.

I picked up a corner of my sandwich and stared at it. Stan was out for my blood. Going over to his house would be suicide. I thought about Sunday when I'd have to go back to church so that Paul wouldn't kick me out of the house. I hadn't gone in months. I'd rather face a thousand Stan Raffertys than spend an hour in that place. Stephen's parents would be there, and I knew as soon as I saw the backs of their righteous heads, I'd want to scream at the top of my lungs that they were ruining our lives and that God saved the fieriest pits of Hell for people like them and not for people like me.

"Hey, Betty Crocker," I joked. Jude looked up from separating the frozen cookies. "Do you think it's possible to buy a miracle? I need one by Sunday."

He looked straight at me. "Save your money," he signed. "They've already been paid for."

Jude went back to placing the cookie dough on a baking sheet, leaving me to digest what he had just said along with my sandwich. Jude never wavered in his faith, and I wondered if maybe I had wavered too easily. It was killing me not having Stephen around, but still, I hadn't lost him completely. Somehow, I'd get him back. I doubted that the Raffertys or even Paul or Luke knew what it felt like to love someone the way I loved Stephen or he loved me. It was easy to feel like my life was falling apart, but maybe I was actually the lucky one.

After finishing my lunch, I reluctantly took the plate of warm cookies and followed Jude to Stan's house. I knocked loudly on the front door and handed the cookies back to Jude. "Here you go, Mother Teresa," I said. The door creaked and opened a few inches. Mrs. Rafferty peered through the crack, and when she saw that it was us, she opened the door the rest of the way.

"Hi, Mrs. Rafferty," I said. "Jude wanted to give you something."

Jude held out the plate of cookies in front of him like an offering.

"Well, aren't you boys just the sweetest things. Please, come in."

We followed her inside the darkened hallway to the living room, where Stan was watching TV.

"Turn that thing off, Stanley," she said. "We have company." Stan looked up. I leaned against the doorway with my arms crossed, trying to look cool.

"Jude baked us cookies. Isn't that sweet?"

Stan rolled his eyes at his mother and started chuckling.

"You boys sit down on the couch while I go get us some lemonade," said Mrs. Rafferty.

She left the room, and Stan got up from his seat. "Trust a princess like you to bake cookies."

"Jude wanted to do something nice for your mother," I said between gritted teeth. "You should try it sometime. But I guess you're too busy these days with your new job, huh? Anybody overdose on your watch yet?"

"Shut up," he hissed. "You're *so* gonna regret this, Peters. And besides, who are you to judge? You think you're family's so perfect, well it's not. You have no idea."

I was about to ask Stan what the hell he was talking about, when Mrs. Rafferty walked in with a tray of lemonade. Stan eased back in his chair, glaring at me. Mrs. Rafferty handed us each a glass.

Stan turned to Jude. "Hey, Mom," Stan said roughly.

"You know all that gardening crap that belonged to Dad? Maybe Jude here would want it."

"Stanley!" exclaimed Mrs. Rafferty. "What a wonderful idea. Why don't you take Jude to the garage and let him pick out what he wants?"

"My pleasure," he said.

Stan was up to something, but I had no idea what. Stan got up, and as I turned to follow him, he pushed me onto the couch.

"Don't worry, Simon," he said. "I can handle this."

Jude smiled at me and trailed after Stan.

I wasn't convinced. I was going to go with them anyways, but then Mrs. Rafferty started talking to me. "My husband wasn't much of a gardener," she said. "He had some big plans for our yard and bought all of these tools, but he never opened most of them. I guess I should take them back to the store, but I'd rather Jude have them. He is such a sweet boy."

"Thanks," I said, not really meaning it. Mrs. Rafferty went on and on about how nice it was that we visited her. An eternity later, Stan and Jude returned. Jude was beaming as he held up a plastic bin full of tools and old gardening magazines.

"What took you guys so long?" I asked.

"Your bro and I were just getting better acquainted," said Stan. "You two may be twins, but Jude here is definitely a lot more fun."

I didn't know why Stan was pretending to be nice to Jude, and I didn't like it. "Well," I said, rising to my feet. "Time for us to take off. Thanks for the lemonade, Mrs. Rafferty."

"My pleasure, dears," she said. "Hope to see you again soon."

"Absolutely," I lied. I didn't want to start making this a habit. I grabbed Jude's arm and pulled him out of the house. As soon as we were on our own lawn, I took the bin from his hands. "What did he say to you?" I asked fiercely. "Did he make you do something or *agree* to do something?"

Jude shook his head. He reached inside the bin and proudly showed me a brand-new trowel that was still in the package.

"You'd better be telling me the truth," I said. "Because Stan Rafferty is no good and he never will be and you *can't* trust him. You got that?"

Jude just smiled and started making digging motions with his new trowel.

I shook my head. He just didn't understand that people could be dangerous. Jude trusted too much and so when it came to his own safety, he was the most dangerous person of all.

CHAPTER 7

Somehow my hanging out with Tina on Sunday night had turned into a "date" and my brothers and Lydia were all excited.

"Oooooh, how cute," Lydia cooed. She sounded like Monique.

Lydia fussed over my hair and made me change my shirt twice. "You're hopeless when it comes to girls!" She huffed. "I'll have to take you under my wing."

I didn't like the idea of being taken "under the wing" of a vulture like Lydia. I was liable to lose an eye.

While Luke and I were doing the dishes after dinner, he slipped something square and plastic into my pocket. It was a condom. "What's this for?" I asked.

"I'm not suggesting anything," he said. "I just want you to be careful. Tina can be a wild one sometimes and we don't need any more trouble, ya know? We got more than our fair share of that already."

"I *can* control myself," I muttered.

He put the last of the plates away in the cupboard. "Some good your control did Stephen," he said quietly. He tossed the dishrag onto the counter and walked away. I wanted to defend myself but decided it wouldn't make any difference. I wasn't going to let Luke ruin my night out.

I sat on the hall stairs by the front door waiting for Tina. My brothers and Lydia were watching some reality TV show. I could hear Tina's car before I could see it coming down the road. I raced to the door.

"Bye guys," I called. "Don't wait up."

Tina's car sputtered to a stop in front of my house, but I didn't recognize the man who was driving or the woman sitting next to him. Tina was in the backseat, so I climbed in beside her.

"Hey, Simon," she said. "This is my sister Angela and her boyfriend Chris." They both smiled at me and said hi. Angela had black hair and porcelain white skin like her sister. "Chris is chauffeuring us around because I have no intention of being able to walk by the end of tonight, let alone drive."

"Guess I'm on Tina watch tonight," I joked. I was glad I was with her this time and wouldn't be getting a call at two in the morning, asking me to come get her from whatever club or bar she had gotten herself stranded in. One night she called me from New Orleans and I had to borrow Luke's truck and drive four hours to a sketchy strip club on Bourbon. Tina had no idea how she'd even gotten there.

We drove through my neighborhood, past the Stop 'n Save, beyond where my old house used to be, out into the country. We took an exit off the highway that I'd never noticed before and turned onto a dirt road. Almost out of thin air, the Toucan appeared on the right. Cars were parked around the building and in the field across the road. There was a large wraparound porch where all different kinds of people were stretched out on plastic lawn furniture. Folks with pink hair, afros, and mullets, men in linen suits and leather-clad bikers. We passed a deep marsh that hummed with insects. The maiden cane rustled in what little wind there was to relieve us from the heat. Chris turned into a driveway covered by a canopy of overgrown trees. I felt as if we were driving into a huge mouth. At the end of the long driveway was a stubby log cabin with an old Chevy truck parked out front. Chris stopped the car behind the truck, and we all got out.

"It's like an all-you-can-drink buffet." Tina laughed.

Chris and the girls went up to the door and knocked. I followed behind. I heard a shuffling inside and the door swung open. A heavy man with long, braided white hair appeared in the doorway. He wore baggy jeans held up over his belly by red suspenders. He let out a great, deep laugh when he saw us.

"We're baaaack," sang Angela.

"I can see that." He chuckled. "Come on in, kiddos." He ushered us into the house, saying hello to everyone by name until he came to me. "And who might you be?"

"Oh, sorry, Stone, this is my good friend Simon," said Tina.

"Hi . . . ah . . . Mr. Stone," I said.

He laughed. "No misters here, kid. The first name's Stone, and that'll do. Have a seat, everybody, and tell yer old uncle Stone all the news from town."

Uncle Stone? Tina never mentioned that this old pirate was her uncle.

We walked through the small hallway into a sitting

room with big soft chairs and a large stone fireplace. The floor was covered in thick shag carpet, and at one end of the room there was a retro looking bar with a red counter. All that was missing was a disco ball and some go-go dancers. Stephen would have gotten a real kick out of this place.

"I'll be right back," said Stone. "Make yerselves at home." I sat down next to Tina on Stone's couch.

"You didn't tell me this guy was your uncle," I whispered.

"*Great* uncle," she corrected. "Yeah, he's my gram's brother, but they haven't talked for years. She doesn't exactly approve of his line of work, if you know what I mean."

"Oh," I said. "Well, at least you have a cool uncle."

"Yeah, Stone's the best. Angie and I can drop in whenever we want and have a drink with him and talk. A person like him isn't the judging type."

Angela and Chris climbed into a big recliner and cozied up together. I couldn't help but be insanely jealous of them. Forget public displays of affection, I wasn't even allowed to *see* the person I was in love with. I think Tina could tell what I was thinking. She leaned against my shoulder.

"We boyfriend-less loners have to stick together," she whispered into my ear.

I guess she wasn't sure if her sister knew about Stephen. I had to laugh though. "When are you ever without a boyfriend?"

Playfully she pushed me against the arm of the couch. "I told you I dumped that jerk, remember?" she said, pretending to be insulted. "I'd totally snatch you up in a second. Sure you wanna bat for the other team?"

She blushed a little and looked away. I felt this strange swirling in my stomach. I liked that she would pick someone like me over other guys. I liked that she was blushing over me. I found myself looking at her the way I did when I met her for the first time. Her tiny shoulders, her slender body, her wrists that were as thin as the neck of a Coke bottle, her round chest. She was perfect, like one of those ivory-skinned mannequins in the department stores.

Stone returned with a tray of mason jars. "Here we go," he said, handing each of us a glass. "This here's the real thing. It'll put hair on yer chest, no question."

Chris turned down the glass and went into the kitchen to get a beer. I sniffed the clear liquid and made a face that Stone must have seen, because he started laughing. "Just open yer throat and swallow," he said. "Hooch isn't for everyone."

I didn't know for sure, but I got the impression that he didn't think I could handle it. I'd never bothered competing with my brothers in sports or in their living-room wrestling matches, because I knew I didn't have a chance. But by not trying, I became the weak one, the *girlie* one.

Tina was sipping on her drink like it was Kool-Aid, not saying anything about the awful taste. I didn't want her to think I was some wuss. I raised the glass to my lips and took a long drink. It burned my tongue and throat, and I couldn't make out any particular taste, just pain. I pulled the glass away and saw that it was half empty. My eyes were watering, and I wanted to run into the kitchen and drink all the water from the tap, but I held my ground and looked straight at Stone.

Stone was smiling. "Yer okay, kid," he said. "You know good stuff when you see it. This guy yer boyfriend, Tina? 'Cause I like 'im."

Tina and I looked at each other. I was surprised she didn't immediately say no. She didn't say anything, in fact.

"We kind of are together at work." I chuckled. "See, we have a little prank going on with this girl who keeps trying to set me up."

Tina smiled faintly and took a sip of her drink. Then she looked down at the floor as if she was disappointed somehow.

"So you's just friends?" he asked.

"Well, yeah," I said. "Best friends." This made Tina smile again.

Stone nodded and took a long drink without even flinching. "My three wives, my three *ex*-wives, were all friends too at one time. Yer smart, don't ruin it."

We drank our hooch in silence, until Angela started talking about the downtown and how it was becoming even more deserted. "You two were smart to get jobs at the Stop 'n Save," she said. "Lovely Ladies is the last store on the block still open. I'll be lucky if I don't lose my job."

I looked up. Lovely Ladies was the clothing store where Lydia worked.

"Do you know a girl named Lydia?" I asked.

"Sure," she said. "You know Lydia?"

I nodded. "Yeah, she's my brother's girlfriend."

"No way!" Angie squealed. "What a small world! Isn't it great about the baby?"

I nearly choked on my moonshine . . . not like that was hard to do. Tina and I looked at each other in shock. "What?" I asked.

"You don't know?" Angie said, confused.

"No, I had no idea!" I was almost shouting. "How long has she been . . . you know?"

"Not long," she answered. "She's not showing or anything. She just told me earlier this week, like Monday or something."

I leaned back into the soft chair and downed the rest of the horrible tasting liquid.

"I'm sure they were gonna tell you soon," Tina said.

"Oh my God," whined Angela. "I'm *so* sorry. I should have kept my big mouth shut."

I looked at Stone. I could see where he got his name from. He was smoking a cigarette now with a blank expression on his face.

"Don't worry about it, Angela," I said. "I would have found out eventually."

Angie reached for Chris's hand, and he kissed her on the top of her head to make her feel better. They looked really happy together, and I could feel the pain moving from my mouth to my chest.

I was leaning against my locker, dreading going home. I had flunked an algebra test and Mrs. Oliver wanted the test paper signed by one of my parents and returned to her by Wednesday.

"Who died?"

I looked up to see Stephen.

"Nobody, man, I failed a test. I'm so dead."

"Come on, Simon," he said. "It's just one test. Who cares?"

"My parents will," I replied. "I have to get them to sign the damn thing. As if failing isn't embarrassing enough, that witch Oliver wants everyone else to know about it too."

Stephen stood beside me and reached down for my hand. He had never touched me in public before, especially not at school.

"I'll go with you," he offered. "I think your mom has the hots for me anyways."

I groaned and gave him a gentle push into the locker next to mine.

Stone asked us if we wanted more to drink, and I jumped a little in my seat.

"You kids don't have to drink any more of that stuff if you don't want to. I got plenty of beer to go around."

And he did. Stone kept handing us can after can while he drank cup after cup of his homemade brew. I'd never gone out drinking before, and I was kind of embarrassed at how quickly I felt lightheaded and blurry-eyed. Tina, this ninety-pound little girl, was pounding them down like Cherry Cokes. The more she drank, the more she floated, waving her arms around, hanging her head on my shoulder, cozying up to me. Tina and her sister were flirty drunks. Angie and Chris were making out right in front of Stone, which creeped me out. But Stone didn't seem to notice. He was a happy drunk, swaying in his rocking chair, laughing at jokes he must have been telling in his head because he said very little.

"Hey, you should be celebrating!" Tina exclaimed. "Yer brother the saint knocked up some girl. You're in the clear now. He's got no right to say anything bad about you anymore. Nada."

I hadn't thought about it that way, probably because the Captain was always on a moral pedestal with me groveling at his feet. It was like he thought he was immune to temptation or sin, that those were only *my* problems. Tina swallowed the rest of her beer. Stone was looking at her with a sad face.

"I think you kids should be gettin' on home. It's late."

Chris pulled himself up and grabbed Angie around the waist, practically lifting her out of the chair. As I stood up, the room started to spin but then straightened out. Tina was holding her own better than Angie. She got up from the couch and filled her arms with empty cans. I grabbed the rest and followed her into Stone's kitchen, where we threw them into the garbage can under the sink. As we walked to the door, Tina stumbled over her own legs. She started giggling. I grabbed her arm and helped her the rest of the way. Stone was waiting in the hall. Chris and Angie were already outside walking to the car.

"Thanks for comin'," said Stone. "You kids make an old man feel young again."

Tina wrapped her arms around Stone. "See ya soon," she said. "Real soon."

I followed Tina out of the house, my hands braced in front of me in case I had to catch her again. "Thanks, Stone," I said, but the old man didn't seem to hear me. He had this faraway look in his eye, as if there was something really fascinating in the woods beyond us.

"Hey, Tina," he called. "Say hello to yer grandmother for me, will ya? Tell her . . . tell her old Stone's thinkin' about her, the stubborn old girl."

Tina nodded and waved, and I looked behind me to

see Stone leaning in the doorway with what looked like a lifetime of regret in his liquor-stained eyes.

Tina fell into the backseat, and Angie was half asleep in front of me.

"Looks like it's just you and me, bud," said Chris. It was the only time he'd spoken to me since we first said hello.

"Yeah." I laughed. "Tina wasn't kidding. Does she drink like this a lot?"

"Enough," he said.

Enough, I thought. *Enough what? Enough to forget about her brother, her grandmother? What was enough*, I wondered, *for Tina?*

"I'm gonna drive back to the trailer and drop off Tina," said Chris. "You stayin' over or do you need a ride home?" The car clock said it was after one, and I didn't want Chris to go out of his way. Besides, I was tired and just wanted to sleep. I'd stay at Tina's and set her alarm so I'd be back at the house before Jude woke up for breakfast. I'd just have to splurge on a cab if Tina didn't feel like driving me.

"Yeah, I'll just stay over."

"Cool," he said. "That works."

We were silent the rest of the drive back to town. I stared out the window thinking about what Paul's baby would look like. A little baby Captain. Nothing good could come from Paul and Lydia. Not together, anyways. I felt sorry for the kid already. His mother would be on his ass all the time, and his dad would have his whole life planned out before he even took his first breath. He didn't have a fighting chance.

The Toucan was still busy when we drove past, only the noise was much louder now that everyone had been drinking for a while. I wondered if Stone ever went down to his bar to drink with his customers like he drank with Tina, Angie, and Chris. I wondered if the folks at the Toucan made him feel young too.

Tina suddenly tapped me on the shoulder. I turned away from the window. She looked much more awake than she had when we'd left Stone's cabin.

"You okay?" I asked.

"Hmmm," she sighed, stretching out her arms. "Sure am."

"Listen, if it's all right with you, I'll crash on your couch tonight," I said.

"Yeah, that's fine, but believe me, you don't want to sleep on the couch. I can hear my grandma snoring even with the bedroom door closed."

"Oh. Well, we'll figure something out."

"You can stay in my room," she said. "Angie's going home with Chris anyways." She sounded irritated that Angie wasn't coming home with her.

"Hey," I said. "I'm stickin' around. You'll see. You and me, we'll be at the Stop 'n Save together 'til we die."

"And Tobey," she added. "That kid's a lifer."

"Yeah, and Tobey too."

She smiled and reached for my hand, and I let her take it. Chris turned on a country western station, and we listened to Brooks & Dunn and Trace Adkins the rest of the way to Tina's house.

The trailer park was on Zion Road, just off the highway. Technically it had been renamed Mayor Long Boulevard, but everyone switched back to calling it Zion Road when Long was arrested three years after he retired for tax evasion and money laundering. The little homes seemed to stretch on forever in the dark. Chris stopped in front of Tina's double-wide manufactured house with pale blue paneling.

"Thanks for being DD, Chris," said Tina, as she flopped out of the car. "G'night, sis."

"Thanks," I said. "It was nice meeting you guys."

"You too, man," said Chris. Angie was still asleep and made a sniffling noise. I followed Tina up the stairs to the front door. She turned to face me.

"Shhh," she said with her finger on her lips. "We have to be quiet. Gram's sleepin'."

She grabbed the collar of my shirt and lured me inside the dark house. She kept pulling me, and I nearly tripped over my own legs, or they might have been hers, I couldn't be sure. Tina was giggling, quiet at first and then much louder, and I had to tell *her* to be quiet. She struggled over the door handle to her bedroom, but once we got inside she let go of my shirt, now stained with sweat, and flipped on the lights. She stood in front of me with a strange expression on her face. Suddenly, she pulled her pink T-shirt over her head and tossed it on the floor. She was wearing a white bra with tiny bows where the straps started. I couldn't help but stare. She walked toward me, pulling the straps down.

"Simon, do you think I'm pretty?" she asked.

She kept walking, slowly undressing as she came closer to me. Her shoes, her socks, her jeans, everything. I knew what she wanted, I just didn't know why. I turned away, embarrassed.

"Tina, you're drunk. I don't think this is such a good idea."

"I do," she said. She was standing right behind me. "You didn't answer my question." Her soft breasts were pressed against my back, and their touch sucked all of the air out of my lungs. I couldn't move, let alone speak.

"You've never been with a girl before, have you?" she asked, knowing full well that I hadn't. I shook my head a little. I felt scared and stupid for not knowing what to do. But I *wanted* to know what it was like. I thought of Stephen and felt guilty for even considering the idea of cheating on him. But Tina was suddenly pulling up my shirt. She was too short to lift it over my head, so I pulled it off for her. Any guilt I felt was now overpowered by her hands fiddling with my belt and pants zipper. Once they were around my ankles, I kicked them away with my foot, and there I was like Tina, like the day I was born. She grabbed me around the neck and brought my face down to hers. We started kissing, and I could taste strawberry on my lips. They were deep kisses that seemed to swallow our entire mouths. We fell onto the bed. Her skin was so soft. I felt her legs, her back, her arms. Perfectly soft. Not a single hair or bump or scar. She pulled up suddenly.

"You don't have one, do you?" she asked. At first I didn't know what she meant. Have what? But then I remembered what Luke gave me.

"In my jeans pocket," I said.

She giggled. "*Simon*," she teased. "I'm impressed." She jumped off the bed and rummaged through my jeans until she found the little packet.

"Relax," she said. "You have no idea what you've been missing."

I lay on Tina's rumpled bedspread, trying to catch my breath. The rush of pleasure had worn off and the reality of what we had just done was hitting me like a punch in the stomach. I didn't know who I was anymore. Or *what* I was. Tina was lying beside me. I could hear her breathing and see her chest rising up and down from the corner of my eye. I sat up and looked down with embarrassment at myself, at the shriveling plastic thing hanging off me. I got up from the bed and took a Kleenex from Tina's bedside table. I removed the condom and after wrapping it tight in the Kleenex, I threw it in the pink garbage can with disgust. I searched around the dark floor and found my clothes. The room felt like an oven, the air heavy, and it was hard to breathe.

Tina had covered herself with her red bedsheet. That great Choctaw pride had drained from her eyes. "Do you love me, Simon?" she asked.

"Of course," I answered. And it was the truth. I'd do anything for her. She turned over on her side to face me and held her head up with her hand. I threw on my shirt and zipped up my pants. I looked around for my shoes. I found them by her bedroom door and struggled to put them on.

"No, Simon, I mean are you *in* love with me?"

Oh Tina, I thought. *Please don't make me choose.* I looked into her sad eyes, wanting to love her like she wanted me to. I was angry at myself. She was beautiful and interested in *me*, and how perfect we would look together. She would sit next to me in church and everyone would say how they'd been all wrong about me. And Jude, who loved Tina, would live with us, and we'd be even happier than when Mom was alive. We'd be the perfect family, except for one thing. Stephen wouldn't be there. He'd be in that place, and by pretending to love Tina I would be betraying him as much as myself. I wanted that perfect life, but it would never be mine and neither would Tina, no matter how much I wanted her to be.

"Good night, T," I said and closed the bedroom door behind me as I left.

I hitchhiked back to my house. An old hippie van stopped for me just outside the trailer park entrance. A young couple was in it with a one-year-old baby girl named Rosebud. I sat in the back of the van on top of a cardboard box. They were traveling evangelists, they told me, on their way to a convention in Baton Rouge, but they were stopping here for the night. They asked me if there was a Motel 6 nearby and if I had a personal relationship with the Lord. I told them I did, absolutely, and that the closest motel was the Golden Nugget, which was only five, maybe ten minutes from my house. I felt like slime around these good people. I reeked of beer, and I only hoped that it masked the stench of sex that I knew evangelists could smell even if I couldn't.

They dropped me off in front of number twelve like I had asked, and I gave them directions to the motel.

"God bless," they called as they drove away.

I unlocked the door and went inside. The house was dark and silent. Everyone was asleep. I walked slowly up the stairs, but the quieter I tried to be, the more the stairs creaked. I slipped into my room and pulled off my sweaty clothes. I put on some clean boxers and got into bed. Jude was sleeping. He had the fan on high to cool down the room. I lay in bed with the fan blowing air in my face. I couldn't stop thinking about Tina, who was probably crying and certain that all guys really were creeps. Luke had been right. I couldn't control myself, and I couldn't stop hurting the people who meant the most to me. I wanted to see Stephen again more than anything, but how could I look him in the eye after what I'd just done? I thought of the traveling evangelists, and I wished that I had just kept driving with them to that convention in Baton Rouge where they would dip my head in holy water and make me new again.

CHAPTER 8

I woke up before Jude did that morning. There wasn't really much to wake up from. I'd sleep for a few minutes, be startled awake by a nightmare, and then couldn't remember what it was about. Over and over this happened. My head hurt pretty bad and while I wasn't sick to my stomach from the beer, I was from the guilt of having betrayed two people I really loved.

Jude was still asleep, and I hesitated before going downstairs and seeing everyone else. I didn't know if I would be able to keep my mouth shut. I had a dirty little secret, like ammunition burning to be released. I wondered if Lydia had told Paul about the baby. I guessed she probably had. It would explain his horrible mood recently.

Luke and the others had to go to work and were in the kitchen eating breakfast. Luke was tossing back a few Stop 'n Save brand toaster pastries with a coating of hard, fluorescent blue icing.

"Hey!" he shouted, spewing blue crumbs. "The man of the hour! How was yer date?"

"It was great," I said casually as I poured myself some coffee.

"What'd you guys do?" he asked.

"Yeah, Simon, out with the details," prodded Lydia.

I thought about Lydia having a baby, and it seemed so ridiculous that if I didn't know it was true, I wouldn't believe it possible. "Nothin' special," I said. "Actually, we just hung out at her place and watched some movies. I met her family, though. Nice people."

"I still can't believe you nabbed a hottie like Tina Kingfisher," said Luke, nudging me with his elbow. "She wouldn't happen to have a good lookin' older sister, would she?"

We both laughed, but then I looked at the Captain who was sitting back in his chair reading the paper with his nose stuck up in the air. He thought he was so goddamn perfect. "Actually, she does," I said. I looked at Lydia. "Her name's Angie. Cute like Tina." I could see something in Lydia's expression change. "She works at that clothing store of yours, Lydia. Small world, huh? Yeah, she was a real interesting girl. Had some real interesting things to say too."

Luke mumbled something, but I wasn't paying attention to him. I was watching Lydia. Her eyes became huge with fear. She knew that I knew. She had to. Lydia kicked Paul under the table and motioned to the door.

"We'd better get going," she said.

Paul looked down at his watch. "But it's only—"

"Paul," she interrupted. "We'd *better* get going." The Captain didn't bother to argue and rose from his chair.

"I got some work I have to take care of tonight," he said, "so don't wait up for me for dinner, all right?"

I nodded, and after they'd left, a little smile crept across my face. For once I was enjoying the feeling of having the upper hand.

I was off most Monday nights, but I wanted to see Tina at the store during her shift. I waited outside, watching her through the huge windows until she went on break. I had left Jude putting a jigsaw puzzle together at the kitchen table with Luke. When Tina left her register, I went inside and followed her. I walked right into the ladies' locker room. Lucky for me no one else was in there. She didn't seem surprised to see me.

"Are you stalking me, Simon Peters?" she asked. She had that little smile back on her face.

I laughed a little, but it was a forced laugh. "Listen, Tina—," I began.

"No," she interrupted. "Don't. We were drunk. Let's just pretend it never happened."

"But it did happen."

She shook her head. "Yeah, well, if it had meant something, Simon, you wouldn't have left, would you?" She was fiddling with the combination to her locker.

"I thought we were pretending," I said. "You know, because of Monique and stuff."

She shook her head and chuckled, but she wasn't laughing, not in a good way. "I know, but I guess I thought maybe you were confused or something. What a joke, right? What a fucking joke. I mean, what was I doing falling for a guy like you, when I knew all along that you're . . . ?" She stopped suddenly. Not even she could say out loud what she was thinking in her head, like if she refused to actually say it, it wouldn't be real.

Tina finally opened her locker and reached inside. She pulled out a black leather book the size of a large photo album. "Here," she said, handing it to me. "It's a scrapbook for Jude. I've been waiting for them to go on sale."

"Really? Thanks, he'll love it."

"Good," she replied. "Tell him I want lots of drawings and lots of poems."

"I will," I said, looking down at the floor until I couldn't stand the awkwardness between us. "So how bad is this?" I asked. "You think we can fix things?"

"Don't be such a drama queen," she teased. "Of course we can fix things. I'll just have to come up with a creative and ever-so-slightly painful way for you to make things up to me."

"Oh, well, as long as I have something to look forward to," I joked.

Tina laughed and sat down in a yellow plastic chair, the kind they have in primary schools. She smiled and nodded her head toward one of the other chairs. I chose the one that didn't have a huge crack in the seat. Despite the fact I was in the girls' locker room, I stayed and talked with Tina for her entire thirty-minute dinner break. She chewed on a peanut butter sandwich she'd brought from home and a Kit Kat bar she'd stolen off the impulse buy shelf at her register. A couple of ladies came in, but no one seemed to care I was in there.

Tina looked up at the large black clock over the door. "I . . . ah, listen, I have to go," she said. "Break's over."

She rose from her chair, and I followed her out of the locker room and back to the front end. Tina walked behind her register, and customers peered around the rows of candy bars and magazines, waiting for her to open.

"I'll see ya tomorrow, okay?" she said.

"Yeah, see ya." I turned to leave. Something was holding me there, looking at her; something that I needed to say. "Tina, you know how you asked me last night if I thought you were pretty? Well, the truth is, I think everything about you is beautiful. Everything."

It was strange, the expression on her face. I couldn't make out if she was happy or sad. I don't think *she* even knew.

I left the Shop 'n Save and walked through the muggy summer night looking forward to sitting on my bed in front of the fan. I had to go through the strip mall parking lot, past the Burger Shack and the Pilot Café, to Gibsland Street. The parking lot was almost empty except for a few cars parked outside the twenty-four-hour Burger Shack. As I approached Gibsland Street, I saw a skull-and-crossbones bumper sticker on one of the two cars left in the parking lot. I examined the car and its plate from a distance. I recognized it quickly. It was Mrs. Rafferty's car, but the bumper sticker was all Stan. I slipped behind a row of trees that lined Gibsland's sidewalk and looked carefully over at the abandoned pharmacy. I could just make out Stan's body leaning against the building. There was another man standing in front of him. I got as close as I could so as to get a look at the other man. I recognized him immediately. It was was Roger. He worked for Mr. Perrucci and was one of the Captain's friends. My heart started pounding loudly. Stan pulled a small, clear bag from his backpack and handed it to Roger. Roger examined the powdery white contents carefully. I couldn't believe how obvious the whole thing was. Talk about an amateur.

"This stuff's more expensive than what I get at work," said Roger.

"Better quality," Stan answered.

"Come on, Stan," Roger said. "It's from the same stash. You just get my buddy to push it for you."

"Okay, fine," said Stan. "You can have it for three hundred. But I'm gonna have a word with my associate and prices *will* be goin' up."

Roger was beaming. "Thanks, man. I *really* need this. You have no idea." He reached into his pocket and pulled out a roll of bills. He slid them over his fingers as he counted them and handed a pile to Stan.

"It's always a pleasure," said Stan. "You Perrucci boys are good customers." The two of them started walking back to their cars.

"Will I see you next week?" Stan asked, opening his car door.

"I don't think so," Roger answered. "It's a lot easier to get it at work. The little lady asks me too many questions when I take off this late, ya know?"

"That's fine," said Stan. "You know who to see when you need another hit."

Roger got into his car and went speeding through the parking lot. Once he had driven away, I came out of hiding and started walking down Gibsland Street toward my house.

Now I knew all of the rumors about Stan dealing drugs were true. Not only that, he was selling to Perrucci's workers on job sites. How was Stan getting onto those sites? I don't know what triggered the thought. I had no proof, but at the same time I had this nagging feeling Paul was involved somehow. He was Perrucci's trusted right-hand man, Roger's "buddy," and he needed the money, especially with a kid on the way.

I took a deep breath and picked up the pace. *I don't have time to worry about this*, I thought. *Whatever Paul's up to, it's not my problem.*

I spent the rest of the walk home trying to convince myself I actually believed that.

CHAPTER 9

When I left for work on Saturday, Jude was working on the scrapbook Tina had bought for him. I had a short shift that day from noon to five. As I was leaving, I noticed a couple of letters sticking out of the mailbox. I was about to toss them inside the house when I saw some familiar printing on one corner of a white envelope. I took it from the pile to get a closer look. It was from Stephen. I frantically ripped it open. There was just one page of notebook paper inside, and the shortest note he'd ever sent me.

> *Dear Simon,*
>
> *Things are going okay here, but it's pretty boring without you. I figured I would have heard from you by now. Did they send you away too? Not that you'd be able to tell me if they did. You probably won't even get this letter.*
>
> *Stephen*

I folded the paper and slid it into my pocket. For the first time, Stephen sounded as if he was losing hope; losing hope in me. But what was I supposed to do? If the Center screened his calls, wouldn't they also screen his mail? Of course they would. Besides, I wasn't going to come clean about the huge mistake I'd made with Tina in some dumb letter. Stephen was going to have to hold on a bit longer until I could figure out a way to visit him.

I arrived at work almost on time and went straight to the locker room to change. Saturdays were so busy that both Renee and her boss, Jeb, came in. Jeb was leaning up against the supervisor's desk when I walked to the front end.

"Mr. Peters," he said, glaring at me. "You're on six. Chop chop, you're late again." I didn't waste any time. I turned quickly and went straight to my register. It wasn't long before a line of customers formed.

Time dragged on, and it didn't help having Jeb snooping around my lane whenever I didn't have any customers. I really don't know what trouble he thought I could get into in one of those tiny cubes.

After my shift was over, I walked by the butcher shop to see if Mannie was working. Mannie and I had taken the new employee orientation class on the same day and we'd discovered that we'd both applied for jobs at the Stop 'n Save to help keep our families together. Mannie's mother had Alzheimer's and needed lots of extra care that was crazy expensive. If I came by the butcher shop, he'd slip me whatever he could—usually the older cuts of meat he was going to get rid of anyways. He was behind the counter elbow deep in ground beef. He smiled when he spotted me.

"One minute," he mouthed and then disappeared. I wandered around the area, checking out packages of meat as if I wanted to buy something. Mannie came out from the back a minute later with a large paper bag. "Steaks," he said. "Real beauties too."

"Thanks," I replied. "This will be a nice change from mac 'n cheese."

"No problem, kid. Now get out of here before someone sees ya."

I took Mannie's advice and left before Jeb caught me loitering around. When I got to our house, I walked into the living room and found everyone watching a sci-fi movie on TV.

"Hey, y'all," I said, but no one looked up but Jude. "I got us steak for dinner." That got their attention.

"Steak!" shouted Luke. "From Mannie?"

"Yup. Fresh and juicy. I take it you guys didn't make anything already?"

Lydia giggled as if I'd said something ridiculous. "*Us*? Cook? Nah, we were gonna order pizza or something."

"You guys will have heart attacks by the time you're thirty," I said. Lydia had packed on a few pounds since I'd met her, but that probably had as much to do with a baby on the way as her crappy diet.

Jude and I went into the kitchen and he helped me put some food together. I threw some seasonings on the steaks and turned on the burner under Mom's skillet. Jude put on a pot of water, and I watched as he carefully cut up some potatoes. While the potatoes were boiling, I fried the steaks with some onions. By then Luke had pulled his lazy butt off the couch and had set the table in the dining room. I defrosted a bag of hamburger buns I found in the freezer and mashed up the potatoes. Once all the food was ready, Paul and Princess Lydia emerged from the living room. They sat down at the dining room table like royalty and waited to be served.

Luke swallowed a huge bite of steak and looked over at Jude. "Tell everyone what that lady on the TV said about fig trees."

Jude put down his knife and fork so that he could sign. "She said that the tree of the knowledge of good and evil was a fig tree, but I already knew that." He immediately picked up his fork and started eating again.

"But I thought it was an apple tree," I said. "Didn't Eve give Adam an apple and then shit hit the fan?"

Luke started laughing, and Paul glared at me.

"Don't swear," he said crossly. "And you're right, it was an apple tree. That lady doesn't know what she's talking about."

"She was on the Bible Network," Luke said and winked at Jude. Now, it was Luke's turn to get glared at by Paul.

Jude chewed his steak calmly. He put down his fork and began to sign again. "In Latin the word for apple is spelled m-a-l-u-m, which is very close to the word for evil, spelled m-a-l-u-s. So it's possible that Christian monks who translated the Bible are the reason that the tree of the knowledge of good and evil is thought to be an apple tree."

We all just stared at him, but inside I was grinning from ear to ear. I loved it when Jude showed everyone how smart he was, and I especially liked it when he proved Paul wrong.

"Well, that's real interesting," said Paul, "but there's no proof it wasn't an apple tree." That was pretty typical of Paul to ignore facts that were right in front of him.

Luke got up from the table with his plate and cup and announced that it was time for ice cream. "Do we have any of that cookies and cream stuff left?" he asked me.

"No," I said, "but I got a new thing of chocolate." Lydia was up out her seat and into the kitchen at the mention of chocolate. She came back a few minutes later with five ice cream sundaes on a tray. She took Paul's empty plate and placed a sundae in front of him. We'd just started eating when Paul pulled the pager off his belt buckle that his boss had given him a couple of weeks ago. He'd told us Perrucci gave it to him because the old man relied on him so much.

"I have to go," he said. "I forgot that I . . . ah . . . have some business to go over with Perrucci."

"On a Saturday night?" squealed Lydia. "But you promised me we'd go to Justin and Kelly's tonight, remember? It's her birthday!"

"Well, you'll have to go alone." He kissed her on the top of the head and left the room quickly. None of us moved. A few seconds later, we heard the front door shut and he was gone. Luke thought nothing of it and dived right into his ice cream. Lydia crossed her arms and sulked. It seemed strange to me, Paul jumping up and leaving like that. I stood up and looked out the dining room window. I could see the street and part of the Raffertys' front lawn. Paul was standing on the sidewalk talking to some bulky guy. He had his back to me so I couldn't see his face. Paul gestured with his arm, and they started walking toward his truck in our driveway. The man turned. It was Stan Rafferty. I squinted to make sure I was seeing what I thought I was seeing. No one would believe me, but this looked like proof that Paul really was involved in Stan's drug dealing. The truck backed out of the driveway and drove out of sight.

"Yer ice cream's melting," said Luke, slurping more sundae into his mouth.

I sat back down at the table. Luke and Jude polished off their sundaes and went into the living room to watch TV. Lydia left the house without even a thank you for the free dinner. I was left sitting in the dining room by myself, swirling melted ice cream around with my spoon. Paul, who had control over everything our parents left us, was sneaking around like some criminal. To make matters worse, I remembered that tomorrow was Sunday. Paul was kidding himself if he thought that the parishioners at Cross of Calvary wanted to see me back at church. It wasn't only because I hadn't gone into sex rehab, which meant I was refusing to change my deviant ways. It was my presence in general that stirred up anger and fear in them, as if I was doing it all on purpose. I wanted them to understand that I had no desire to be the object of either their hate or their fear.

"Do you believe all that stuff Pastor Ted says about sexual immorality and going to Hell?" I asked Stephen.

He was sitting on his bed, making a face at a math problem he'd been working on for the last fifteen minutes. I was supposed to be working on the next problem so we could swap answers, but my mind had been wandering, as usual.

"Dunno," he said, continuing to stare down at the page. "I used to. Now I have no idea. Hey, are you done with number seven?"

I couldn't believe how unconcerned he sounded. "This is,
like, our souls I'm talking about here, Stephen. Who cares
about trigonometry?"

Stephen raised an eyebrow at me over his textbook. "Mr.
Weeks does," he replied and chucked a pencil at me. "So
focus. We'll worry about our souls some other time."

A film had formed over the ice cream, so I took it into
the kitchen and washed it down the sink. I wondered if it
was my soul that the parishioners at Cross of Calvary were
worried about, or if it was their church's perfect image
that Stephen and I had marred.

CHAPTER 10

There were at least seven different kinds of churches in our little town: Catholic, Episcopal, nondenominational, Lutheran, Baptist, Methodist, and Pentecostal. Most of the parents at the Cross of Calvary didn't want their children to be corrupted by exposure to other kids from other religions, or worse yet, "secular" kids, so most of them homeschooled their children. Before Jude had his problems, my dad wouldn't let us be homeschooled. "Over my dead body," Dad said, "are *my* kids going to turn into a bunch of mama's boys."

He loved that expression, *mama's boy.* He'd smack Paul on the back or wrestle with Luke on the living room floor. He never said anything to me about being small and liking to read or play Mom's piano. He never said a word but he had a special so-what-the-Hell-went-wrong-with-you? glare that he would send my way.

Even though I would have rather pulled out my wisdom teeth, I got in the truck with Paul and Lydia to go to church. Luke followed behind us with Jude. I sat in the back and prayed for an asteroid to hit the interstate.

It had been months since I'd last walked into the gymnastics school that had been converted into a huge church. There were no bells, no signs, no impressive stone walls; nothing to make it look like anything other than an outdated gym. Despite this, the parking lot was full and people were pouring inside. The Cross of Calvary Church was a new-age kind of church filled with young families and teenagers. Our services were aired on TV stations all over the state, which made us by far the coolest Christians on the block.

The Cross of Calvary attracted those who didn't want to stand up or sit down all the time reciting old prayers from dusty books. The fashion label in this place was Jesus the Big Man Himself, and the kids my age were proud Jesus Freaks. WWJD was on their hats, their shirts, their shoes, and even etched permanently into their skin. But my brothers were proof that the "What Would Jesus Do?" gear didn't make you a good Christian. Paul acted like a virgin and pretended that he and Lydia were waiting for marriage. He thought that Jude couldn't figure out what was going on behind the closed bedroom doors, but one afternoon Jude had stuck his index finger into a circle he'd made with his thumb and forefinger to let me know that they'd been at it. Now that Lydia was knocked up, Paul was going to get his wedding sooner than later. Luke was definitely not waiting for marriage. He went through girls faster than boxer shorts, dropping them without bothering to say good-bye. Even so, I was the one who had been picked out as the pariah, the one who liked guys in a disgusting way.

The thing with Stephen had changed everything for me at Cross of Calvary, but the truth was that I would have done anything to fit in with everyone the way I had when my parents were alive. I knew that was impossible. As I walked into the chapel with my brothers and saw the people who had once been my friends and who now wanted to change me or simply couldn't look me in the eye, I wished I could melt into the floor.

Paul led us to seats in one of the middle aisles. I guessed it was better than sitting in the front, but not nearly as appealing as the very last row. I hated walking past those hypocrites who wanted to know every detail of what Mr. Lévesque saw when he caught me and Stephen together. I'm surprised he didn't do a Powerpoint presentation.

Instead of pews, there were rows of red chairs. They were designed especially for the church, complete with a little metal loop where you could place your empty cup after Communion. We never went up to the altar to kneel for Communion; we had servers pass around baskets of Matzo bread and round trays with tiny plastic cups filled halfway with grape juice. We did this because we didn't *have* an altar to kneel at. I guess that would have been too mainstream.

I sat down next to Jude. As I studied the church newsletter, I felt people's stares burning into the back of my neck. Whenever I looked up, I could see people glaring at me, their faces asking *What are* you *doing here?* I didn't recognize some people, and they were the only ones who looked at me without reproach. A couple of my parents' old friends who were bigwigs in the church came up to say hello to Paul. "Simon's here today?" I heard someone ask. Their voices became whispers as they nodded their heads toward me.

I began scanning the congregation, looking for the two people that I wanted to avoid the most. I needed to know where they were so that I could plan an escape route when the service was over. They were seated in the far right corner of the third row: Mr. and Mrs. Lévesque, Stephen's parents. Losing them had been like losing my own parents all over again.

Mr. Lévesque had put his hand on my shoulder, but it wasn't until I'd turned around that I even realized he had. I'd been sobbing uncontrollably as they lowered my parents into the ground. I couldn't feel anything but the pain, so Mr. Lévesque tightened his grip so that at least I would feel him there next to me.

"You're gonna be okay, Simon," he whispered. "You've got a bigger family than you think."

Mr. Lévesque wasn't the overly emotional type, but he was strong, and on the day of my parents' funeral he had been strong enough for both of us. The Lévesques even hosted the reception at their home afterward so that my brothers and I wouldn't have to worry about cooking and cleaning up.

My chest started feeling tight like I couldn't breathe. I had to look away. I couldn't understand how two good people could send away their only son like he was some hopeless junkie. Maybe someday they would see that Stephen wasn't a lost soul or a degenerate. He was a martyr.

People quieted down as the Praise Team, which was made of up a guitarist, a pianist and a drummer, began to play "King of Glory." Afterward, the president of the church's board, Mr. Kimble, kicked off the service with a short speech and an update of church events.

"Hey!" he shouted.

"Hey!" echoed the congregation.

"Now, now, we can do better than that. *Hey*!"

"Hey!" repeated the congregation, only louder.

"Much *better*!" he said enthusiastically.

Mr. Kimble launched right into the announcements. The Married Couples' Bible Study would be meeting at the Weavers' house on Tuesdays instead of Wednesdays and the nursery still needed more volunteers. He closed by reciting Romans 6:23: "For the wages of sin is death, but the gift of God is eternal life in Christ Jesus our Lord." He emphasized the word "death" by raising his voice and pounding his fist on the podium.

Pastor Ted was now up at the front beaming at everyone. He was sporting his usual floral print Hawaiian shirt. The cameramen focused in on him so that the service could be aired throughout Louisiana. Before the pastor started his sermon, we stood and sang while the worship team played the drums, guitar, and piano in the background. The lyrics were transmitted onto two large screens at the front of the room. The congregation sang loudly, clapping their hands or raising them high into the air. I mumbled the familiar lyrics.

> *And blessed be Your name*
> *When I'm found in the desert place*
> *Though I walk through the wilderness*
> *Blessed be Your name.*

After we sang three songs, Pastor Ted asked everyone to sit down. Like I did most Sundays, I floated in and out of Pastor Ted's sermon.

It was hard to give him my full attention as he rambled on about one line of scripture for twenty minutes. He spoke for a full hour with no breaks. Mostly, though, I just didn't want to pay attention. I knew that I was in trouble when Pastor Ted announced that he would be reading from Revelation Chapter Two. All that seven seals and apocalypse stuff was a little heavy for Pastor Ted.

"Nevertheless, I have a few things against you," his voice boomed as he read from the Bible in front of him. This woke me from my daze. "You have people there who hold to the teaching of Balaam, who taught Balak to entice the Israelites to sin by eating food sacrificed to idols and by committing sexual immorality."

I waited for it and then it happened. He looked at me, just for a split second, as he was saying that last part about immorality. I knew he would, and I stared back at him. I could not change who I was. I could hide it or lie about it, but I could not change something that I had no control over.

I blocked out the rest of the sermon by reading the church bulletin over and over. When Pastor Ted was finished, we all stood up and sang a few more songs and then the service was officially over. My eagerness to leave could only be compared to when you really, *really* have to go to the bathroom. Paul and Lydia were talking with some friends who had sat beside them and after fifteen minutes of waiting, I started to get anxious.

"I gotta get out of here," I whispered to Jude. He walked down the row toward Paul and tugged on his shirt.

"It's after twelve and I'm hungry," he signed slowly so Paul could understand him. "I always eat lunch at twelve."

"Well, you heard the little man," said Paul, who was surprisingly not annoyed. "Let's go, gang." We piled out of the chapel into the building's main hallway. Luke stretched his long arms over his head.

"I was dying in there," he said to me. "I usually get through Pastor Ted's services by staring at Jessica Todd's chest, but she wasn't here today."

We both laughed, and he put his arm on my shoulder and shook it gently like he was trying to wake me up. "See, man," he said. "No one's perfect."

I was almost out the door, just steps from freedom, when I saw Mr. and Mrs. Lévesque at the double doors to the parking lot. They were shaking hands with the parishioners and blessing them as they left for the day. I had never seen them do this before, but I could only guess that after what happened with Stephen they had to work extra hard to keep up appearances at church. I turned to Luke in a panic.

"What do I do?" I whispered. "I can't talk to them."

"Just stand behind me," he said, grabbing my arm. I fell into line behind Luke and kept my eyes down. I could see Paul shake Mr. Lévesque's hand, but they didn't say anything to each other. Lydia smiled and hugged Mrs. Lévesque like they were best friends. Jude, oblivious as usual, walked right past them.

Sorry," said Luke to the Lévesques. "Jude doesn't mean to be rude."

"Not to worry," said Mr. Lévesque with a laugh. "He's a good boy." He shook Luke's hand as Luke moved toward the parking lot.

I found myself in front of Mr. Lévesque for the first time since he had caught Stephen and me a year ago in our clubhouse. I had my shirt on this time, but I felt as naked under his glare as I had that day. We stared at each other. Mr. Lévesque's lips were drawn tight like he was actually afraid to talk to me. Maybe he was afraid of what he might say. I reached out my hand. Without even hesitating, he turned and began to speak to the person standing next to me. "Simon," hissed Luke, "come on, everybody's waiting."

I dropped my hand and followed Luke outside. No one spoke very much on the way home. Luke told a joke and we laughed a little, but only to be nice.

"It's not your fault Stephen's in that place," Paul piped up. "The Lévesques just can't accept that they screwed him up."

I knew that Paul was wrong, but I didn't feel like arguing with him. I blamed the Lévesques for sending Stephen away but not for making him gay. No one was at fault for that, because there was nothing to be at fault for. I didn't ask to be this way. Who would ask to be an outcast? Maybe it was easier in some places, but not here. I wanted to believe that God wouldn't test me more than I could handle. That if I was meant to overcome the way I was, I would have done so by now and Stephen would have too. I hoped that I was right. I just didn't know for sure if I was.

CHAPTER 11

I hid in the back of the garden under the cover of the fig tree for the rest of the afternoon. The tree had grown fast, but as trees go it was still just a baby, and its short canopy covered me when I sat right up against the trunk. Jude put a beach towel on the grass near where I was sitting and worked on his scrapbook. My whole body was itching from what had happened at church, and I couldn't seem to sit still. He looked up at me and smiled.

"Why did Stephen's parents send him away for being happy?" he signed.

I snapped out of my daze. "What? Jude . . . no, they didn't send him away because he was happy. Well, I mean he *was* happy, but they sent him away because something made him happy that's against the rules."

"But you said he was gay," he signed. "Like in the Flintstones song."

"What?" I asked. But then I remembered the familiar lyrics to the theme song about having a "gay old time." I couldn't help but crack a little smile. Jude took things so literally. He didn't know any other meaning for the word "gay," and I didn't have the energy to try and explain it to him. Anyway, I didn't want him knowing. I couldn't bear it if he thought badly of me or Stephen.

He came toward me with his scrapbook and opened it to a page filled with smiling stick figures. He had drawn little circles like halos over some of their heads. One of the characters was bigger than the rest, and he held the hands of two smaller figures that stood next to him.

"See," Jude signed, pointing to the larger person at the center of the picture. "Here is Stephen, and you and I are beside him." He pointed to other figures on the page. "And here is Mom and Tina and Luke. We're all together in the happy place, with Stephen."

I could feel myself choking up, so I swallowed hard, burying the thick loneliness I felt without Stephen. "That's nice," I said. "Stephen would like it a lot."

He smiled and closed the book, rubbing his hand up and down on the cover. He liked the way certain things felt.

"What is that thing that is against the rules?" he asked.

"Being himself," I replied.

"Being yourself is against the rules?"

"Yeah," I answered. "Sometimes it is."

Jude put his scrapbook down and was staring at the house with a contemplative look on his face. "Paul breaks the rules too, doesn't he?" Jude asked.

I nodded. "I guess if you're the 'man of the house,' you can do whatever you want," I replied.

"That's not fair," he signed.

"No, man, it isn't, but you know what? Karma gets you every time."

"Is he in trouble?"

My lips curled into a smile. "He got Lydia pregnant," I replied, without thinking. I instantly regretted opening my mouth. "But don't say anything. Paul will flip out."

Jude's eyebrows furrowed, but he didn't respond.

"You hear me, Jude? You can't say anything."

Jude got up and started walking toward the house. The heat was probably getting to him. I assumed he understood. After all, Jude never purposely antagonized Paul. I followed him inside where Luke was eating Stop 'n Save brand cream center cookies.

"You guys want some?" he asked.

Jude shook his head, but I took a couple. We all went into the living room, and Luke and I watched *Revenge of the Alien Brides* on TV while Jude worked on his scrapbook and did some crossword puzzles. It was after ten when I heard the Captain's truck pull into the driveway. I thought about how he went off with Stan Rafferty the night before, and I had this feeling of déjà vu. I went to the living room window and pulled down a few sections of the blinds. Paul was coming toward the front steps, and Stan was walking away from the truck. This was the second time in two days. Would Luke believe me now? I doubted it, but I wondered if I should tell him anyways.

I heard Paul close the front door, and then he appeared in the living room doorway. He looked tired; *old*.

"Hey," he said wearily. He eyed me suspiciously when he saw I was standing by the window.

"Hey," I replied. "What were you doing with Stan Rafferty out there?"

"That's none of your business," he snapped. "Don't you remember what we talked about last week?"

Luke suddenly perked up. "What did you guys talk about last week?" he asked.

"That's none of *your* business," answered Paul.

Luke shrugged and started watching the movie again.

"Fine, don't tell me," I said. "Forgive me for asking about your day."

Luke snickered. "When did you ever care about his day?"

"Well, it's just that I saw him take off with Stan last night too."

"You ditched Lydia for *Stan Rafferty?*" Luke asked with surprise. "Damn, you better not tell her that. She'll scream like a banshee."

Paul took two large steps into the room. "I don't *plan* on telling her, and y'all had better keep your traps shut about it."

"Ahhh, you two having problems?" teased Luke. "Or is that wishful thinking?" He winked at me. Luke and I had always hoped that Paul would come to his senses and date someone else. *Anyone* else.

"Lydia and I are fine," he said. "In fact, we're getting married."

"Married?" Luke shouted, as he lurched forward in his seat.

"Yeah," said the Captain. "As soon as we can."

"Where's the fire?" Luke asked.

Paul laughed. "No fire, man. We just love each other and want to get married."

Luke was staring at Paul in complete shock, while I just stood there, not at all surprised. I knew Paul was lying through his teeth about there being "no fire."

"Well, congratulations," I said, not meaning it. "But that doesn't explain what you were doing with Stan Rafferty."

"Stan needed some business advice, that's all. He's really grown up a lot."

Luke's eyes nearly bugged out of his head. "Are we talking about the same Stan?" he asked. "'Cause the one *I'm* thinking of is a little shit who bullies Jude and Simon every chance he gets."

"So Stan is going into construction?" I asked.

"What? No," he said impatiently. "It's something else, but you two wouldn't understand." The way he said "you two" just dripped with condescension.

"Oh, really, and why is that?" I asked.

"Oh, come on, Simon," he said. "Don't take it personally. It's just what would a high school dropout and a car mechanic know about operating a business?"

That did it. Luke catapulted to his feet and pointed a shaking finger at Paul. "Do you have *any* idea why he's a high school dropout and I'm a car mechanic?" Luke shouted. The roar of Luke's voice startled Jude out of his chair, and he flew to the far corner of the room, his hands on his ears. "Well, do you? We did it so we could take care of each other and our brother who can't take care of himself!" His face was dripping with angry beads of sweat and the veins in his neck were bulging. "We make sacrifices for this family while you and Lydia hoard all your money God knows where and do nothing! When was the last time you bought food, huh? Or did the laundry? Or washed a dish for Christ sake? When? You prance around like the world thinks yer pretty, and all you do is judge people! Well, I'm sick and tired of you judging us!"

He turned to me. "Do you know what he says about you behind yer back?"

"Luke, don't," said Paul, with a flicker of fear in his voice. "That's just gonna make things worse."

"He calls you a girlie fag!" Luke shouted. "He says yer a disgrace to the family because of what you and Stephen were caught doing and that yer gonna go to Hell for it! But the yellow belly doesn't have the guts to say it to yer face!"

Something inside of me shrank. I knew that was what Paul thought. I knew that was what other people thought too. But thinking and saying were so different sometimes. Like one was real and the other wasn't. Paul looked at me as if he was genuinely sorry, but I knew he was only sorry for getting told out. Luke's shoulders heaved up and down with each violent breath.

"Come on, guys," Paul begged. "Don't you see what's going on here? All this stress is tearing us apart. Money and bills and putting food on the table." His voice fell to a whisper. "You know it wouldn't be this hard if Jude wasn't so dependent. *He's* the cause of all our problems, not me." I looked at him in disbelief. "Oh, don't look at me like that, Simon. You'd have long since graduated high school, Luke here'd be in premed, and Lydia and I would be married by now and living in a house of our own. Hell, I'd probably have my own company already. Now, don't get me wrong. All right, he's our brother and we love him, but don't ya'll be taking this out on me when I'm just trying to be the adult here and make a life for me and my girlfriend. You can't fault me for that, right?"

I thought I was going to be sick. Jude was so innocent

that any guilt would slide off him like a fried egg on Teflon. If only Paul knew how ridiculous he sounded blaming Jude for our problems.

Luke's whole body was shaking, and he looked as if he was going to cry. His voice was just as shaky. "The way you talk about Simon and Jude, it's like they're aliens or something. Forget about treating them like brothers, you don't even treat 'em like people. Huh? Some Christian. And helping out a creep like *Stan Rafferty*? Man, I don't even know who you are anymore." He pushed past the Captain and ran up the stairs before any of us could see the tears.

The Captain shook his head and glowered at me. "Apparently, I'm not trying hard enough." He laughed bitterly. "Well, that's fine. I can step it up. Just you wait. You'll see how *I* take care of things." It was like he was threatening me and trying to prove himself at the same time. "I'm going to Lydia's." He barged out of the house and slammed the door behind him.

I stood there for a while, too angry to move, wishing God would get back in the habit of smiting people. If I were Him, the Captain would be at the top of my list.

I felt like I was all alone in the room, but I wasn't. I had almost forgotten that Jude had been there the whole time. He was huddled in the corner, his eyes shut tight and his hands glued to his ears. I hoped he hadn't taken in what the Captain said about him being the ruin of all our dreams. I wasn't too worried about the "girlie fag" part. Jude wouldn't have a clue what that meant. I walked over to him.

"Jude," I said, "look at me." I pointed two fingers shaped like a V at my eyes. He followed my fingers and looked at me.

"So much shouting," he signed.

"I know," I said. "But it's over now."

"I'm the reason they shout," he signed. His face was wilting with sadness.

"No, Jude, most of the time it's *me* they're shouting about."

"But I'm the reason you're all unhappy."

I held his shoulders. "No, no, no." I tried to sound upbeat. "*You* have nothing to do with our situation. Understand me? *Nothing*. The Captain was just doing what he always does, you know?" I sat him down on the couch and took a seat on the coffee table in front of him. "Jude, do you remember when Mom took our Sunday School class to the petting zoo to see some of the animals Noah saved on the ark?" He nodded and smiled for a quick second thinking about the animals. "Mom looked around to ask you if you wanted a ride, but you weren't there. You weren't anywhere. She told the rest of the kids not to move a muscle. She started running through the zoo, yelling your name, asking people if they had seen a little boy who was by himself, until she found you at the horse paddock. She held your hand for the rest of the day and wouldn't let you go, remember that? And when we got back to the church, some of the kids told their parents what had happened, and their moms and dads got angry at Mom for leaving the other children alone while she searched for you. But Mom didn't care. She said that any of those parents would have left the group to go find a missing child. Because she knew, like Luke and I know, that without you our lives might be a little easier, but they wouldn't be any better. The Captain just doesn't understand that."

His little smile vanished. "I can't blame him for wanting an easier life," he signed.

But I could. I could blame Paul for ignoring the fact that we went hungry some nights while I waited for my paycheck. I could blame him for allowing me to drop out of school, and I could *definitely* blame him for threatening to kick me out of the house if I didn't tow his Pleasantville line. Sure, I could blame him and so could Jude, but in the end, what would that actually change?

CHAPTER 12

I sat at a booth in the Pilot Café waiting for Tina so we could grab some lunch before work. I also wanted to plan my trip to visit Stephen at the Waverley Christian Center on Saturday when we were both off.

"How are those brothers of yers?" Baptiste had asked when I walked in. "I don't see 'em around much anymore."

"Oh, they're around," I replied.

I had been at the house all morning but hadn't seen the Captain since he'd stormed out last night. Luke was unusually quiet all day and wouldn't even look at me. Guess he felt bad for telling me all of the crappy things Paul had been saying about me behind my back.

In a way, I was glad he did. Everything that had gone down the night before had made me realize that I was stupid for waiting. I had to see Stephen now. I could feel my family, and Stephen, slipping away. Sometimes, I felt as if Jude was all I had. I needed to know for certain that Stephen was going to be a part of my future and not just a part of a past that I didn't want to let go of.

If Stephen had changed and if he didn't love me anymore, then all the rejection and suffering had been for nothing. I could have just said that whole afternoon at the clubhouse was a big mistake or that we'd been experimenting and didn't know what we were doing. But when Paul had confronted me after he found out, I'd told him that it had been more than all that, it had *meant* more. I'd been wrong about plenty of things, but I hoped to God, if He was still listening, I hadn't been wrong about Stephen.

Tina walked in and slid into the seat across from me. "So you're ready to do this thing?" she asked.

"Yeah," I replied. "So what was our deal? If I visit Stephen, you have to go on at least three dates with a guy before sleeping with him."

Tina laughed and kicked me playfully under the table. "Let's keep this conversation about you, lover boy," she teased. "So, how far away is this place?"

"About two hours east," I answered. "Outside Denton, Mississippi."

"Okay, so if we left at one, we'd be back by six or seven," Tina proposed. "If you don't get in we'll be back a lot sooner." I could tell she was expecting me to give her a rundown of my brilliant plan to break into the Center. I didn't have one and my silence answered her question.

"Disguise?" she asked.

"No," I replied quickly. I didn't have a clue how I'd get in, but I did know one thing. "I'm done hiding."

I told my brothers that I had another date with Tina on Saturday. I couldn't tell them the truth, which was that she was taking me to see Stephen. Paul and Luke whistled at me and actually *spoke* to each other for the first time in days when they thought I was going on a second date with a cute girl. The *girl* part being the most important thing to Paul.

Luke offered to take Jude to the arcade and then to Chubbe Burger. He had fixed one of the burger flipper's cars the other day and the guy had promised him as many free burgers as he could eat the next time he went.

While Luke was hunting for quarters for the game machines, Jude pulled out his scrapbook and showed me the page he had been working on. This one was for me, he signed, and he looked very pleased with himself. I was standing on a rock, one of my arms on my waist and the other pointed high in the air. My mouth was a big circle, which I thought meant that I was talking. It looked as if I was in our backyard because Jude had drawn the fig tree, only much larger than it actually was. All around me was a crowd of stick figures. The picture was kind of funny, but I didn't want to laugh at Jude's work. He seemed so proud of it.

"They're listening to you," he signed.

"Oh yeah," I said. "And what exactly am I telling them? That cream soda twelve-packs are on two for one?"

Jude cocked his head to one side the way he did when he was confused. "The truth," he signed simply. "What else?"

I just smiled, having no idea what the truth was. I didn't even know if it existed anymore, at least not in this house.

"Thank you," I said, and I meant it. "What are you going to work on today?"

"Finish your page and start one for Stephen," he signed.

I wanted to tell him that I was going to see Stephen, but I just couldn't risk it.

I met Tina outside the Stop 'n Save. She pulled into the parking lot, and I waved to her. The closer she got to me, the more nervous I became, and by the time I climbed into her car, I was starting to feel sick to my stomach. I managed a quick, "Hey, how are ya?" but my mind wasn't really in the moment. Part of me was dreading seeing him. I was afraid that he wouldn't be the same person. I had wanted to go alone, but Tina insisted that she come along for support, and then she gave another reason that I believed more.

"I want to see you two together," she said. " 'Cause that will kinda solidify the whole idea, ya know? Make it a little bit more real."

I didn't like the idea of Stephen and me being some kind of freak show that people stared at.

"Oh, so did you hear the news from the store?" she asked, interrupting my thoughts.

"No, what news?"

"Jeb fired a bunch of people last night. Bev in sanitation texted me around eleven."

"*What?* How many people? Did she tell you why?" I blurted out.

"Wow, easy killer," she replied. "It was like ten or something, but she didn't know exactly why, the economy maybe. But she did say Jeb made some big announcement outside the locker room that they were cleaning house and anyone who wasn't getting with the program would be out of there."

"Oh, terrific," I said. "Guess the fag will be next."

Tina scowled. "Don't use that word. But yeah, you might be right." She looked worried.

"Hey," I said. "Sorry, don't listen to me. I'm never right anyways."

Her lip curled into a half smile. "Well, that's true," she said. "Here, help me with directions."

She handed me her phone and I entered the address into the GPS. Once we were on the highway and it was pretty much a straight shot to the Louisiana–Mississippi border, I turned down the radio. These layoffs had got me thinking.

"You ever think about college?" I asked Tina. "You've already got your high school degree."

She snickered. "I'm no brainiac, Simon. Besides, what would I do at college?"

"Well, I think you're smart," I said. "When I see you with Jude, I always think about what a great teacher you'd be. You're so patient and good with kids. And you'd be a perfect teacher for the deaf because you already know how to sign."

"You think so?" she asked.

"I know so. And think about it. Teachers make pretty good money and get a whole summer for vacation. How could you go wrong?"

"I'd be the first in my family to go to college," she said. "But I can't afford it."

"Tina, you can't afford not to," I said. "Otherwise you'll be stuck working for Jeb until your back gives out . . . or until he fires you, and then what?"

"Maybe," she said.

"Maybe? That's it? Don't you want to get out of here?"

"Yeah, but so do you and I can't just leave you here."

"Yes, you can," I replied. "Do what the rest of us can't.

Besides, what kind of friend would I be if I just let you stay here and be miserable because I didn't want you to leave?"

"What if we did this together?"

It was my turn to snicker. "Tina, I don't even have a high school degree."

"But you could get it," she said. "Practice what you preach, Simon. You go back and get your GED and my gram can look after Jude while you're in classes."

"Listen, T, I appreciate the offer and all, but it's not Jude." I stared out the window at the brown fields flashing by. "Well, I mean it is Jude, but it's not about who will watch him. It's the money. He can't support himself. He can't even heat up SpaghettiOs without burning himself." I threw up my hands in defeat. "It's so frustrating. He's brilliant, I mean he's the wisest person I know, but he'll never be able to make it on his own. He'll always need help, and what if I'm not around to give it to him? People will just walk all over him."

Tina looked at me with those intense eyes of hers. "Jude will be fine," she said. "And so will you, but only if you start taking care of yourself, for Christ's sake."

"I'll think about it if you do," I compromised.

Tina nodded and turned the music back up.

We made good time and were on the outskirts of Denton in an hour and a half. We drove for another thirty minutes without seeing any sign of human life. The GPS indicated we'd arrive at the Center in an eighth of a mile. A concrete building appeared on our left and looked out of place in the middle of low-cut fields. Tina slowed down and turned into the parking lot of what looked like a decrepit senior home. The kind you read about in the paper where the residents aren't taken care of and are found dead in their rooms.

"He lives *here*?" she asked in disbelief.

"No way," I said. "His parents are snobs, but they'd never leave him in a place like this."

"It says 2400 Route 32. What did you put into the GPS?"

I checked her phone, and my heart sank. 2400 Route 32, it read.

"Just look," she said. "The sign's right there. *Waverley Christian Center.* We're in the right place, Simon."

I shook my head in disbelief. The gray building was like a bunker with small slits for windows. There were about half a dozen cars on one end of the parking lot and the rest of the place was deserted. All it was missing was a barbed wire fence. "This can't be it," I nearly shouted. "It's worse than the loony bin! It looks like a *prison.*"

"But it's the place," she said. "Come on, maybe it's better on the inside."

I doubted it. I got out of the car steaming mad, wishing that the Lévesques' necks were between my sweaty hands so I could snap them in two.

"Well, I can't just walk in," I said. "So, we'll have to find another way inside."

"You could try. How do you know for sure they won't let you see him?"

"They'll have my picture," I replied. "The Lévesques would have given it to staff and told them to never let me near Stephen." I looked around to see if there was a back entrance. "There's gotta be another way."

"Are you serious?" said Tina. "You really think his parents hate you that much?"

"Let's just say it's lucky for me that 'thou shalt not kill' is one of the Ten Commandments."

"All right." She sighed. "So what are we gonna do, scale the walls?"

"There's got to be a kitchen entrance or something," I said. "Come on."

We walked around the drab concrete building where there was a large green Dumpster. A young Latino guy dressed in a white uniform was leaning against it and smoking a cigarette. I walked up to the man and Tina followed me.

"Hey," I said. He looked up.

"Hey," he said with a thick accent.

"Do you speak English?" I asked.

He nodded.

"Listen, I have a proposition for you." He looked confused. I pulled out my wallet and showed him the cash inside of it. "I'll pay you if you can help me," I said slowly. The man nodded and sucked deeply on the cigarette.

"Sì, dinero," he said.

"I need to get to Stephen Lévesque's room," I said even more slowly. "Can you tell me how to get there?"

He was watching my mouth carefully, trying to understand my words. "Sì, sì," he said. "Lo puedo."

"Sì" I could at least understand. "*Gracias*," I said. "Here, this is thirty bucks. *Treinta*." I held the money out, and he put his hand up.

"Be back," he said. He put out his cigarette and walked

inside the building without taking the money. I looked at Tina, and she just shrugged.

"I think he'll come back," I thought out loud. "He said he'd be back." We waited outside for what felt like a long time, but I don't think it was. The man appeared suddenly in the doorway with a big smile on his face.

"Come," he said, and he motioned to us with his hand. Tina and I followed him inside to a white staircase. Below, I could hear the crashing of pots and Spanish curses. The man led us up two flights. He peered around the corners and when he saw that no one was coming, he waved to us and we followed. At the second floor, he stopped us with his hand. Then he opened a steel door and looked around.

"*Bueño*," he said, and he motioned us into a hallway that smelled like bleach and was lined with floor-to-ceiling windows. We must have been at the back of the building, because we definitely didn't see these windows when we pulled in.

"Lévesque," said the man, his hand pointing down the hall. "*Dos cientos y doce.*"

I nodded and pulled the cash out of my wallet. He took it from me, counted it, and shoved it in his pocket. "*Gracias*," he said. Then he turned and walked back down the hall, disappearing into the stairwell. I watched him leave, feeling nauseous. I was the closest I'd been to Stephen in months, but it seemed like it all might disappear in a second, as if he were standing in front of me but was only a reflection or a shadow.

"Simon," Tina said, interrupting my thoughts. "You okay? 'Cause we need to hurry."

"Yeah," I said in a daze. "The guy said he's in two-twelve."

Tina took my hand and guided me through the hallway. I suddenly wanted to let go and run as fast as I could outside, but Tina gripped my hand tightly, and I was grateful she had come with me. We stopped in front of 212, the numbers boring into my eyes. Tina looked at me, but I didn't move. I couldn't. She sighed and knocked on the door for me. I could hear rustling inside the room, and my nerves and excitement and curiosity were more than I could bear. I started going over the conversation in my head. I wondered if I should just go with, "Hey, Steve." Or maybe like, "Stephen, God it's been a long time." Or maybe I should have a sense of humor and come out with, "Steve, man, this place is a dump." I didn't have a chance to decide because the door opened and anything that I thought I wanted to say escaped me. It was his wash-gray eyes, only older and sadder. His sandy brown hair, only longer and rattier. His face, only it was tired and thin. It was him, but it wasn't. I had thought I would say something great and profound. Instead, the exact opposite came out of my mouth.

"Jesus, what did they do to you?"

Stephen's lips, so pale they were almost white, crept into a tight smile.

"Simon?" He said my name like a question; as if he wasn't sure he trusted his own eyes.

"It's me," I said. "I hope not too late." It had been my worst fear that Stephen would hate me for letting him rot in this place. If I were in his position, I think I'd hate me too.

"It's been too long," he said, his mouth now in a full, toothy smile. He seemed on edge, like he didn't know what to do with his arms or the rest of his body. He suddenly grabbed my shoulders in a tight hug, and I hugged him back, thinking that no matter how tightly I held on to him, it would never be tight enough.

"Come on inside," he said with a hint of panic in his voice. "I'm not supposed to have any visitors." Stephen moved aside so that we could come in, and he closed the door quickly behind us. His room was plain but clean. The walls were a bright white, and the only color in the whole room came from two posters of Christian rock groups, the navy blue blanket on his tiny bed, and a framed sign that read *Cast your burden on the Lord, and He shall sustain you.* I looked at Stephen more closely. He was so thin and fragile a strong wind could have blown him over. I couldn't stop looking at him. After a few awkward minutes, Tina nudged me.

"S-sorry," I stuttered. "Stephen, this is my friend Tina from work. She drove me here." Tina smiled, walked a few paces toward Stephen, and shook his hand.

"Oh," he said quietly, with what sounded like disappointment. "Your friend."

"No, no, no, no," said Tina quickly. "Simon and I are *just* friends. I mean, I'm only here because this mooch doesn't have a car." She laughed, but all I could muster was a weak smile. I didn't want her to think that the car was the only reason she was here or that she was less important to me than Stephen. I thought of that night we went to Stone's place and got wasted. Everybody knew Tina had a new guy every week, but I was never meant to be one of them. I was supposed to be the kind of person who said no because it was the right thing to do.

Stephen's face relaxed. "Sorry. When I saw you I just assumed . . . you know, whatever." He sort of laughed. "I don't know what I'm talking about." There was silence as we looked at each other, wondering by the changes in our faces what had gone on over the last few months that felt like years.

"Weeeell," said Tina, "you two look like you have lots of catching up to do so I'm just gonna drive around and, um, see if I can find a 7-11 or something back in that town."

"Thanks, T," I said. "I'll see you soon." She nodded and smiled weakly.

"It was nice meeting you, Stephen," she said and slipped out of the room, checking first to make sure no one was in the hall.

I looked at Stephen again. "I don't know where to start," I said.

Stephen smiled. "How about the beginning. And just go from there."

We sat down on his bed, and the mattress was so thin, I could feel its wires and springs. He lay down with his hands behind his head as if he was about to hear a bedtime story. I let him put his legs over my lap so he could stretch out.

I began to talk, starting at what I thought was the beginning, but ended up jumping around as important thoughts came to my head. I told him about Stan Rafferty and how I was sure he had hooked Paul into his drug dealing ring and how I'd become the Cross of Calvary leper who all of the congregants thought was disgusting.

He listened carefully, licking up every syllable about the outside world. As I explained the constant bullying and my exile from just about everything we had known as kids, the look in his eyes changed, which told me that he understood. When I was finished, I felt exhausted. My hands rested on his jeans just inches from his fly. I wondered if he wanted me to open it. I could feel the beginnings of a hard-on so I caught myself, not letting the thoughts go any further. *That* wasn't why I had come.

"Nice room," I said sarcastically.

"Yeah, Caesar's Palace," he joked. "No roommates, though, which is nice. They think that will cut back on the fooling around."

"So, what is this place?"

"I don't know." He snickered. "One of the janitors calls it a 'fool's errand,' which I guess means that they're trying to do the impossible."

"I'm glad," I said. "I never wanted you to change. Only *they* did."

"Yeah, well, *they've* never bothered to visit," he said bitterly. "Didn't even show up for Christmas. Well, they can kiss my homo ass."

"Forget about them," I said. "They don't matter. Who cares what they want if they don't even have the decency to come see you." I quickly remembered that this was the first time I had visited Stephen, and that I was really in no position to be passing judgment.

"Yeah, I know," he said. "But it's just hard sometimes." He shook his head a little, as if to shake out the bad thoughts. "But, whatever, it's not like this whole thing works anyways. The kid next door to me's been here longer than I have, and nothing's worked for him so he started sneaking in *Playboy* and *Penthouse*, but that hasn't helped either. He showed them to me too, but I wasn't interested. It must be weird to be straight." Stephen was fiddling with the drawer to his bedside table. He pulled out a carton of cigarettes and a lighter. He got up quickly and opened his window. "Want one?" he asked. "If you let the air in nobody can tell. Not that anyone comes in here anyways."

"Sure," I said, hoping it would calm my nerves. He got up and lit a cigarette next to the window and handed it to me. He lit up another and breathed in heavily. By the looks of him, he'd been smoking more than eating the last few months.

I blew the smoke out slowly through one side of my mouth, wondering if I should get everything off my chest. I didn't know how he'd take it, so I just blurted it all out. "Yeah, it is weird," I said. "I had sex with a girl. You know, just to see what it was like. It didn't mean anything, though."

Stephen's eyes became huge. "No way!" he said. "Which girl? That one?" he asked, nodding toward the door that Tina had exited a few minutes earlier.

"No," I lied, trying not to complicate things. "Another one. We were drunk. I mean, whatever. It felt good, but it was like you said, it was *weird*."

He shook his head, but I was relieved to see him smiling about it, as if it was funny. "Man, I can't believe you. I hope you were careful. The last thing you need is to have a bunch a little Simons running around."

"Oh, yeah, that reminds me," I said. "Paul knocked Lydia up so now they're getting married."

"Typical," he scoffed. "Straight people can do whatever the Hell they want."

"Tell me about it," I muttered.

I put out my cigarette in the metal window frame, letting the butt and ashes fall to the parking lot below. Stephen did the same and followed me back to his bed, which was just about the only place to sit other than his wooden desk chair and the cold tile floor. He shook his head. "That's gonna be one screwed-up kid." Stephen sat next to me on the bed and slouched against the wall. "God, I've missed you," he said. "You've missed me too, right?"

"You kidding me?" I answered. "It's been Hell. I worry about you all the time. Nobody will tell me anything, and your letters weren't much to go on, by the way."

"Sorry," he mumbled. "Censorship."

"Did you know it took me almost two months just to find out where you were?"

"I can believe it," he said. "Nobody but you would have cared where I was, anyways."

"So, what exactly do you do here?" I asked, not so sure I really wanted to know. I was envisioning electroshock treatments and hypnosis sessions.

"Oh, it's a blast, let me tell you," he quipped. "Group therapy, one-on-one therapy, scripture therapy, art therapy, you name it, I've done it."

"Do they treat you okay? You've lost a lot of weight."

"They treat me fine," he said with a shrug. "But it ain't exactly home cooking. Hey, do you remember those cheese dreams your mom used to make us with the bacon on top? Man, those were good. I think about those a lot, and other stuff . . . you know, when I'm hungry. So, the garden's doing good?" he asked, obviously changing the subject. "Is that fig tree still alive?"

"Yeah, it's actually getting real big. I thought it'd die, but Jude, well, you know him, he got the green thumb in the family."

"Yeah, he sure does," said Stephen. "I don't know why, but I've been thinking about him a lot too. There's just something about him . . . I dunno, I'm rambling."

Stephen turned his head toward me. We looked silently at each other. It had been so long. Was it okay to touch; to hold each other? Would it be the same? He smiled sort of shyly and then lay down, resting his head on my legs that were dangling over the edge. I ran my fingers through his hair, which felt warm and soft on my hands.

"How long can you stay?" he asked.

"I dunno," I said. I didn't want to leave, but at the same time I wanted us to leave together. To take him away from here and move as far from our town and the people in it as we could. "I shouldn't keep Tina waiting too long," I added. "It was nice of her to come with me at all."

"She seems nice," he said. "Besides I *know* it was her."

"Her what?"

"The girl, stupid. Your little fuck buddy."

"Nice language," I muttered.

"Yeah," he said. "I've picked up a few bad habits in this place."

"You're not mad, are you?" I asked.

"No." He laughed. "I just think it's funny. You were so straight laced; way more than I was." He turned over so that he was lying on his back facing me. "You don't love her, right?"

"No," I answered. "Not like that. I told you it was an accident. I'm still straightlaced, you know, well, sort of." A little smile crept across my face.

Stephen laughed. "Yep, I corrupted you. But you liked it."

"Yeah, whatever, Casanova," I joked. "But seriously, we need a plan to bust you out, 'cause *you're* sure as Hell not staying here any longer."

"Well, I'm eighteen, so I could just sign myself out if I wanted to." He shrugged a little. "My family would never speak to me again if I did."

His words stung my ears. I couldn't believe he could just walk out. Why was he still here? I sort of jumped up in my seat, nearly throwing Stephen off the bed.

"Why didn't you say something?" I asked angrily. "You could have come and stayed with me."

"Yeah, you and your gay-bashing brother," he said just as angrily. "And your piece-of-shit neighbor, that Rafferty kid. No thanks. I had nowhere to go, so I just stayed here. I figured if you came, then we'd work something out, and if not, well, then I'd figure something out myself."

"Goddamnit!" I shouted. "Why didn't you tell me all this in your letters? Did you know that to get in today, I had to pay one of the janitors to sneak me through the back? And all this time you could have just walked out?"

He sat up, his face inches from mine. "You had to *want* to come, Simon, otherwise, how would I know? I needed to be sure that this hadn't scared you off and that I wouldn't be wasting my time."

"Wasting your time?" I couldn't believe what I was

hearing. "We've been best friends our whole lives. You think I'd just take off because of one bad thing?"

"Well, it was a pretty *big* bad thing, Simon. We were caught with our pants down." He let out a chuckle. "Literally."

I didn't find it very funny. "Yeah, but I still can't believe you thought you had to test me. Haven't I proven myself already?"

"Relax," he said, lying down again. "You're here now, aren't you? Besides, I know you tried. It was you who called, pretending to be Todd, the youth pastor, wasn't it?"

I looked down at him pitifully. "Yeah, that was me."

Stephen grinned and rubbed my knee. "Lame, Simon, but very cute."

"That wasn't the only time I tried to call either. So will you come with me?" He didn't say anything, and I knew deep down that no matter what I said to try and convince us both, we couldn't be together, not yet, anyways. "Listen," I started. "Paul and Lydia are gonna want their own place and you know Jude and Luke won't care if you stay with me. Steve, you listenin'?"

"Yeah."

"So, what do you think?"

"What do I think?" He sighed. "I think it's gonna take a miracle for this to work."

We sat there for what felt like a long time, just holding each other. I looked down at Stephen's face. I leaned over and kissed him, breathing in whatever life he had left.

CHAPTER 13

I caught a glimpse of my watch and saw that Tina had been waiting for over two hours. It took all my willpower to pull myself off the bed, but the really hard part was telling Stephen that I had to leave. We tried to act all cool at first as we said good-bye, but then Stephen made this terrible noise, like a whimper. He grabbed me around the shoulders, and I stood there motionless, feeling his hot tears sting my neck. I didn't think I could handle much more. Stephen had always been the strong one, the brave one. I hadn't seen him cry since Max, his golden retriever, died when we were eleven. All of the schemes that got us into trouble as kids were his ideas, and he never stopped thinking up new ones, like the one that landed him in here. He wanted to experiment and go on adventures when I was happy to just stay at home. But he always put up with my whining and never once left me behind.

I pulled away so that I could see his face, which was red from crying. This place had changed him, all right. It had made him give up. I kissed his eye. He leaned in closer, but I pulled back, knowing that if something got started, I wouldn't be able to stop it. I turned the door handle and pushed it open a little, backing up slowly. "It won't be long now," I repeated and closed the door behind me.

I felt vulnerable in that cathedral of a hallway that seemed to go on forever. I could hear voices coming around the corner, so I went straight to the stairs and sprinted down them, hearing my footsteps echo above me. I found the exit by the same green Dumpster. Parked just a few feet away, Tina was waiting for me in her car. She reached her hand through the open window and waved. I climbed into the seat next to her, sitting on a stack of magazines.

"Sorry," she said as she slipped them out from under my butt.

"Don't be," I said. "I'm sorry for making you wait so long." Her car was littered with candy and chip wrappers. "At least you found a 7-11."

"Yeah, took me almost an hour," she complained. "This town's a first class shithole." She pulled out of the parking lot and onto the deserted highway. "So, what are you two going to do now?" she asked.

To be honest, I didn't know. I wanted Stephen to come live with Luke, Jude, and me once the Captain left for good, but Stephen hadn't seemed too sure about that idea. I thought he wanted to get out of our town completely, but since I had to take care of Jude, that was going to be hard if not impossible. Where would we live? I couldn't just transplant Jude to some strange new place. He wasn't that adaptable. We'd moved once before, but it was only across town, and Mom was alive then. Besides, how could I ask him to leave his garden? It was practically his entire life.

"He seems nice," said Tina, interrupting my thoughts. "I *guess* he passes the test." She punched my shoulder playfully and started to laugh, but I just stared out the window. Today was supposed to make everything right again. It was supposed to make me feel better, but it didn't. For the first time I doubted whether Stephen and I were meant to be together. Not because we didn't want to be, but because I had no idea how to make it happen.

"What you need right now is a beer," said Tina. "Lots of beer."

"We're not going to your uncle Stone's place," I said irritably.

She shot me one of her looks. "I'm assuming a house with four guys has a few beers in the fridge. Besides, you don't look like you should be alone."

"Don't worry," I said. "My brothers will be there."

"Oh, okay. I'll just drop you off then."

"No, that's not what I meant," I said quickly. "I want you to come back with me. I just don't see how you can put up with my older brothers."

"I don't think they're so bad. I used to hang out with Luke back in high school," she said. "You're luckier than you think." I shut up after that, realizing I couldn't say anything right. I figured she was talking about her own family, which included a dead brother, a crazy grandmother, and parents who she never saw and never talked about.

We drove the rest of the way in silence, except for Tina slurping her extra-large orange Slurpee. When we turned onto my street, I saw Paul's truck in the driveway. I groaned as I remembered the excuse I'd given my brothers for taking off all day.

"I told them we were on a date," I blurted.

"What? Why would you say that? You know they *know* everything."

"Yeah, but they wish they didn't know everything, so I told them you and I are dating so Paul would get off my back. I think they actually believed me." I looked at her nervously. "So, if you could just, you know, not say anything."

She laughed, but I don't think she thought it was funny. "So, you told your brothers you were on a date with me so that you could sneak off and see your boyfriend who doesn't know that you also slept with me while he was locked away in some religious asylum. *Good job*, Simon."

I kept my mouth shut, not telling her that I'd told Stephen everything, and he didn't care because he knew it hadn't meant anything. "Sorry," I said as we pulled into the driveway behind Paul's truck. "I always mess things up." Tina didn't argue, and I only felt worse when I got out of the car and saw my favorite person standing on his front lawn.

"Hey homo," said Stan, as he walked toward his car.

"Oh, shut up, you big dick," Tina spat. She slammed the car door and went straight inside the house. Stan started laughing.

"Nice, Simone, so now you got girls fightin' your battles for ya." I heard what he said, but I didn't care. The world sucked, and Stan Rafferty was just one tiny smell in a whole pile of shit.

"Where're going, Stanipoo?" I asked with disdain. "Got a hot date with a coke addict?" His expression changed, and I could almost hear the words *oh crap* repeating over and over in his microscopic brain.

"No smart-ass remark?" I asked. "Listen, I hope you're not testing out your own merchandise. I hear it's bad for business and besides, you could use all the brain cells you've got left." I turned and walked up the front steps, finally feeling a little bit better about myself, even though it took tearing down someone else to get there.

"I can't stand that kid," Tina snarled when I got inside.

"Forget about him," I said quickly. "You hungry? Luke's probably started dinner."

"Sure," she said with a shrug. "I've been eating all day anyways. It's good therapy." She walked down the hall toward the kitchen, leaving me to figure out why she needed therapy. Why couldn't girls just say what they meant?

"Tina," I whined. "What's wrong?"

"You know, Peters," she said, without turning around.

Great. She must be PMS-ing, I thought. I often wondered how the Captain put up with Lydia's temper tantrums, and I decided that if being gay meant I could avoid all the female hormonal stuff, then it wasn't me they needed to feel sorry for. I moped behind Tina into the kitchen. Jude was sitting at the kitchen table, and Tina sat down beside him. He was drawing in his book. Luke was pulling something out of the microwave, and a pot of something else was on the stove. He turned around and saw us.

"Hey guys!" he shouted. "How was the date?" I figured by the way he made quotation marks with his fingers when he said the word "date" that he'd finally caught on. "What did you guys do?"

Tina looked at me as if to say, "Don't ask me, this is your lie."

"Oh," I said quickly. "We just grabbed a burger and saw a movie. You know, the spy one."

Luke chuckled. "Burgers and action movies. My kind of date." He winked at Tina, who smiled back at him.

"What's for dinner?" I asked.

"A bunch of things. A TV dinner for whoever wants it, some mac 'n cheese, and I've got a frozen pizza in the oven." He messed with Jude's hair. "Right, kiddo, just call me Emeril." I was about to make a jab at Luke's cooking abilities when I heard the door slam. The Captain stormed into the kitchen.

"Take my advice, guys," he proclaimed. "Never get married." He caught a glimpse of Tina. "Oh, sorry, Tina. I didn't see you."

Tina just shrugged. "You didn't hurt my feelings."

"What she do to you?" Luke asked.

"She dragged me to a florist, a bakery, some store where they make invitations, *and* a caterer. I never want to see pink again."

"You've got a caterer?" I asked, surprised. "How can you afford that?"

"It's my wedding," he answered. "I'm not gonna give my guests coffee and donuts. Besides, we're renting the hall at the church, and everyone will be expecting a good party."

"Yeah, I'm sure they will," I mumbled.

The Captain went to the fridge and started chugging some soda out of the bottle. "So, how was the date?" he asked.

"Good," answered Tina quickly. "We saw a movie."

"On our first date, I took Lydia to a movie, and now we're getting married," he said dreamily. Luke rolled his eyes and put his two middle fingers in his mouth, making a gagging noise. Tina and Luke started laughing, but then they stopped and locked eyes for long enough to make me feel a little awkward. I could have been wrong, but I think my "date" was eyeing my big brother.

"T, do you want to stay for dinner?" I asked her.

She didn't take her eyes off Luke. "Yeah, sure, why not."

Jude tapped Tina's arm so he could show her his book. I grabbed forks and glasses and put them on the kitchen table while Luke hacked at the pizza with a bread knife. He scooped the macaroni into a big bowl. "Who wants this?" he asked as he held up the TV dinner tray.

"What *is* it?" asked the Captain, looking at the brown goo.

"Roast beef and potatoes."

"Hmmm." He shrugged. "Guess I'll take it."

We served ourselves from Luke's buffet and then went into the living room to watch TV. I handed Jude a bowl of macaroni as he sat down in the armchair. Everyone started digging in except for Jude.

"Not hungry?" I asked him.

"He's been in a weird mood today," said Luke. "He wasn't into the arcade at all, and he wouldn't eat anything at Chubbe Burger either." He looked at Jude who was staring down at his bowl. "On a diet, little buddy?" he joked. "Or are you fasting?" He patted Jude on the back and then continued eating his pizza.

"What's wrong?" asked Tina in her sweet voice, but Jude said nothing.

"Just leave him," said Paul irritably. "Don't let him ruin everything."

I glared at Paul, but he was too preoccupied with his roast beef mash to notice me. "I'll make him some toast,"

I said and left the room. I figured he was just mad at me for leaving him all day. I put two pieces of bread in the toaster and leaned up against the counter. I didn't realize how exhausted I was. I think I would have fallen asleep if I hadn't been startled by the Captain's shouts bellowing from the next room. I stumbled out of the kitchen. The Captain was standing over Jude whose eyes were glued to his macaroni. Paul's head looked like a rocket about to take off.

"What happened?" I shouted. My heart was pounding.

"Jude told Luke about the baby," Tina whispered.

Jude looked up at me with a strange expression on his face. "Sorry," he signed. But the damage had been done. Luke and Paul were staring each other down, and I could tell by the looks in their eyes that this time fists might start to fly.

"You're really something else," Luke sneered. "You give Simon a hard time and then you turn around and get that slut pregnant? Well, do us all a favor, Paul, marry her and get the Hell out of our lives!" He pushed past the Captain. "Looks like you're the screw-up this time." There was dead silence until we heard the front door slam.

"I should go," whispered Tina.

I nodded, not knowing what else to do. "See you later," I whispered. She touched my arm as she passed me and smiled a little.

"Jude," I said cautiously. "Why don't you go outside? I think I saw some weeds in one of the flower patches." There were no weeds, but Jude knew better than to argue with me at a time like this. He got up and walked out of the room, his arms dangling at his sides. Paul's face was stony.

"You knew all this time and you didn't say anything?" he asked.

"Yeah," I replied. "But I think Lydia knows I know."

"She never said anything to me."

"She knows you're stressed enough as it is." I suddenly felt bad for him. I guess because I had been in his place. I knew what it was like to have your own family turn on you. "Don't worry about Luke," I added. "He's just mad. He didn't mean what he said, and I know he won't go shooting his mouth off either."

The Captain nodded. "You're not such a bad kid, Simon," he said. "I know I was hard on you, but it worked. You and Tina are good together and pretty soon you won't even remember who Stephen is."

I probably should have seen that coming. Whenever Paul came under fire, he changed the subject and reminded somebody else of their own mess-ups. He shook my shoulder a little, his sign of approval. He dropped his hand like it felt heavy and walked to the door that led into the kitchen.

"Hey," I said. He turned to look at me. "It's no big deal, anyways. Babies are good, right? They sort of make up for everything we've done wrong."

He looked away, staring through the window into the front yard, and nodded a little. He turned and slipped through the door. "I hope you're right," he said just above a whisper.

I was glad that Jude's strange mood wasn't because I'd left him all day. He said he was distracted, but by what, he wouldn't say. We lay on the grass, which was hot and spongy underneath us. I noticed a small green bulb, the beginning of a fruit, on the fig tree's highest branch. The tree had been growing new leaves for a while now, the five fingers of each leaf reaching to the sky. I pointed out the fruit to Jude, thinking he'd be excited, but he already knew about it.

"I saw the fig last week," he signed. "When it was the size of a marble."

To be honest I wasn't all that interested in the fig tree. "Jude, why did you bring up the baby when I told you not to?" I made sure that my voice sounded more curious than angry. "I mean, we all say things sometimes that make Paul mad, but it's not like you to provoke him."

"No, not provoke," he signed.

"Then why?" I asked. "If you had just kept quiet, we might have had a little peace for once. Now Luke's really pissed. Are you mad that they're having a kid or something?"

"No," he answered.

I sighed with frustration. "Okay, I guess you're not in the talking mood."

"I need to see how he reacts," he signed.

I looked at him like he was crazy. "We all know how Paul reacts," I said. "He gets really, really mad and makes life miserable for all of us."

He smiled, which made me even angrier. Why was he smiling? He'd made a big mess that *I* was going to have to fix.

"Because it shouldn't be a secret."

"What's so bad about secrets?" I asked him.

"They're things you're ashamed of. That's why you won't talk about Stephen."

"How do you know about that?" I whispered.

He smiled. "I'm not deaf," he signed. "And I'm not stupid either. I hear people talking all the time."

"I never thought you were stupid," I said quickly. "I know how people talk. I guess . . ." I felt my head rolling back and resting against the fence. "I guess I just didn't want to believe you knew."

"Why not?" he signed. "I'm your brother."

"Yeah, well, so is the Captain," I said bitterly.

He grabbed my shoulder so I would see his face. He looked hurt. "But I'm your twin," he signed.

"I know!" I shouted. "And that's *exactly* why I didn't want you to know. So that you, of all people, would actually respect me."

"Why wouldn't I respect you?" he signed. "Who am I to judge? I knew you were different just like I knew I was different. I'm not like Paul and neither are you."

I watched his hands carefully, processing what he was trying to tell me, and I couldn't believe I had ever been mad at him. He knew this whole time. While the Captain threatened to kick me out and old friends stopped talking to me, he knew and didn't say a thing. Other people would bring it up, even Tina did. They would say it didn't bother them, but the way they talked about it or looked at me made me feel like I was on display. But Jude never even mentioned it. He genuinely didn't care. Maybe he thought being gay wasn't so much a choice as an existence, not unlike how mutism was a part of his existence and not Paul's or Luke's. But at the time his reasons didn't seem all that important. I felt a heaviness sinking away from me that had been there for so long, it had become part of me. There was nothing I could do to change the Captain's opinion or the Lévesques' or Stan Rafferty's. But Jude's opinion mattered.

I put my arm over his shoulder, and he seemed to relax. "How about some ice cream?" I asked.

He smiled and nodded eagerly.

The kitchen was as hot and humid as outside. I grabbed the ice cream from the freezer and stood in front of the cold air for a few seconds. Jude placed two plastic bowls on the counter and got a spoon for me. As I was scooping out the ice cream, he tapped me on my shoulder.

"So, everything is all right now," he signed.

"Yeah, of course it is," I answered. I reached into the cupboard above our heads and took out the bottle of chocolate syrup and handed it to him. "Nothing's changed. I'm still your no-good brother."

Jude opened the bottle cap and meticulously drizzled the chocolate syrup back and forth over the ice cream. He clicked down the lid and placed the bottle carefully on the counter, making sure the label faced straight ahead.

"Do you remember the drawing I made for you in my book?" he signed. I did remember. How could I forget? I was talking to a big crowd. Telling them something important, he had said. "You're the rock, Simon," he signed, not looking up from the bowls of ice cream. "You can't forget it."

I never appreciated Jude more than at that moment. I didn't have to pretend to be someone else for him to respect me as a person, which was all I really wanted. I could make Paul and the parishioners at Cross of Calvary respect me again, but it would cost me Stephen, and that was just too high a price to pay.

CHAPTER 14

The next morning Jude asked me if I was going to church with them, but I think he already knew the answer. I wasn't gonna go looking for trouble. The Captain must have stayed over at Lydia's house because he didn't come down for breakfast. That was fine with me. Just before Luke went upstairs to get ready, I blurted out that I was going to go to Christland Baptist with my manager, Renee.

He gave me a funny look. "Say what?" he asked. "Isn't that a black church? Who says they'll even let you in?"

"Renee says," I answered. "She's been inviting me for months." He stared at me for a few seconds, making sure it wasn't some sort of joke.

"Well." He shrugged. "Just don't get yourself shot. That's not exactly the best part of town." I wanted to tell him we didn't exactly live in the best part of town either and that he should be more concerned about the drug dealer living next door, but I didn't want to start another fight. "I'll be careful," was all I said.

"I'm glad you're going," Jude signed. "I'd rather go with you, but that's not fair to Luke."

"You're right," I said. "He'll be mad if we leave him alone with Paul and the prima donna."

After breakfast we all got dressed. Luke was wearing jeans and Jude was wearing khakis, but I had to wear decent clothes to Christland. I borrowed one of Dad's old suits from Paul's closet. It was a faded navy blue and fit better than I thought it would. When I went back downstairs, Luke whistled at me.

"Hey there, good lookin'," he joked. "Dressed up with nowhere to go?"

"Shut up," I said. "There's nothing wrong with wearing a suit to church."

"Sorry man. It's just, wow, you look like an idiot."

"I'm no more an idiot than those hippies at Calvary who hold hands singing "Kumbaya" like God's some kind of camp counselor."

Luke smiled. "Fair enough," he said. "But at least us *hippies* don't have to wear a tie." He smacked me playfully on the shoulder, causing a puff of dust to fly off the old jacket. But I didn't care how loose or dusty the old suit was. I felt important in this suit because I was going somewhere important in it.

I sat in the back of Luke's truck fidgeting nervously. Maybe Luke was right. Maybe Renee just invited me so I'd feel like less of a reject. What if she never expected me to show up at all? I'd be the token white kid and just like at Calvary, everyone would notice me because I was different. Luke stopped the car a full block away from the church.

"If you change your mind, we can just keep driving

and no one will even know you were here," he said. "What ya say?"

The offer was kind of tempting. Luke could drive me back home and I could go back to sleep or sprawl out on the couch and watch TV. I couldn't remember the last time I had the house to myself. But I also knew that I had come here for a reason. That I had put on this dusty suit in the hopes of getting something back that had been taken from me. "No thanks," I said, as I opened the car door. I had my faith to find.

I could hear the rumbling of the truck long after my brothers had driven out of sight. I walked slowly down the block toward the crowd of people gathered on Christland's lawn. The houses on the street looked like the ones in my neighborhood with white plastic paneling and sunken front porches. The ladies wore summer dresses and some of the men were in three-piece suits despite the heat. My suit itched like crazy, especially around my neck where the stiff collar wouldn't stop scratching. I loosened my tie a bit and undid the top button of the shirt. It wasn't like I was going to win the best dressed award anyways.

I kept walking, trying to act like I knew what I was doing. I scanned the faces for Renee and her family, but I couldn't see them anywhere on the church lawn. *Great*, I thought. I was gonna have to go in alone. I decided I'd walk on the edge of the lawn and then cut across once I got near the front door. A few pairs of eyes were watching me curiously, but as soon as I stepped on that lawn, it was like I had crossed into forbidden territory. Every conversation stopped dead as I passed by, with pair after pair of eyes trailing after me. They all looked more perplexed than angry, except for a couple of old ladies who glared at me suspiciously.

The large oak doors were open and welcoming. *Once I get inside I'll be okay,* I thought to myself. *I'll find Renee and sit down low in one of the back pews and no one will even notice me.* My pace quickened, but as I crossed the lawn to enter the church a tall brick wall of a man walked quickly toward me. His shoulders were as wide as the church's double doors, and with his long legs he beat me to the entrance. He jumped onto the front steps, blocking my way. *Oh God,* I thought in a panic. *He thinks I'm one of those white supremacists who plants bombs and shit in people's churches.* I stopped a few paces from the steps so that I was out of reach of his Mike Tyson arms. I was ready to turn and bolt when he surprised the Hell out of me.

"Are you lookin' for someone?" he asked with a smile. My mouth fell open and I couldn't bring myself to answer. "You're new around here, aren't you?"

"Ahh, sort of," I managed to stutter. "Actually, I'm looking for Renee Badeau. Is she . . . ah . . . here somewhere?"

The big man's grin widened and he walked down the stairs next to me. "He knows Renee!" the man shouted to the people who were watching us like we were actors in a play. A murmur suddenly swept over the crowd, as they finally knew why the strange white boy was at their church. "How do you know Renee?" he asked.

"She's my boss," I answered, a little more relaxed.

"Oh, okay," he said. "You work at the Stop 'n Save?"

"Yeah, don't remind me."

A corner of his mouth curved into a grin. "The name's Lewis," he said. "And yeah, I know where Renee's at. Follow me."

He motioned inside, and I followed him through the heavy oak doors into the large, bright chapel. There was no stained glass in the church, but it did have tall windows stretching from the floor to the high ceiling. Dark wooden pews lined each side of the chapel and next to the pulpit was a statue of Jesus with his arms stretched out in front of him. The minister was talking with a few kids who looked about my age. His long white robes gleamed against his dark skin. I watched them laugh and joke around like the pastor was just one of the guys. Pastor Ted liked to be all buddy-buddy with the church's teens, especially the guys. He loved to show off how much he knew about cars and sports. I remembered when I used to be included in those conversations.

I watched Lewis scan the chapel. His eyes finally rested on a group in the far right-hand corner of the church. Children were running around the pews, and I saw Renee's daughter duck underneath one as if she were playing hide-and-seek. I noticed John, Renee's husband, first because he towered over the other parishioners. Renee stood next to him, almost as wide as she was tall. She looked so relaxed, not at all like how she seemed at the store.

"Right there," said Lewis, nodding in her direction. "I'm sure she'll be glad to see ya."

"Thanks," I replied. I began walking slowly toward the group, hoping Lewis was right and that she *would* be glad to see me. Suddenly Renee's eldest daughter, Ashandra I thought her name was, crawled out from underneath a pew in front of me. She looked at me curiously.

"I know you," she said.

"Hi, Ashandra. I'm Simon, I work for your mom."

She giggled. "I'm not Ashandra. *She* is." She pointed her little finger to Renee's other daughter who was now standing in the pew next to her sister. "*I'm* Mariama," she said proudly. "It means gift of God."

"Oh," I said. "You both look a lot different from when I last saw you."

This seemed to make Mariama happy, as she puffed out her chest a bit and smiled, revealing a large gap between her front teeth. "I've grown *three* inches this year and now I'm the tallest girl in my class," she stated proudly.

"Wow," I said. "The *tallest* girl. That's great."

"Do you want to see Mommy?" she asked.

"Yes, I would," I answered.

"Come on."

I let her take my hand and lead me closer to where her parents were talking with their friends. I have a picture in my memory of Renee's face when she first saw me. The warmest smile I'd ever seen. "Siiimooon!" she squealed. I let go of Mariama's hand just as Renee grabbed me in a tight hug. She pulled back just enough to look at my face. "I'm so glad you came," she said. "This is *just* what you need. Come on, sugar, let me introduce you to my family."

She guided me over to the group of people she'd been talking to. Renee introduced me to her two sisters, Janette and Sheri, and to her brother, Jeff. Her sisters were with their husbands and the little kids running around with Ashandra and Mariama were theirs also.

The piano started up with a quick, jazzy song, which seemed to signal the rest of the crowd outside to come in. Without saying anything, Renee and her family started drifting toward a middle pew. I tagged along at the back next to Renee and Mariama.

"This is a nice place," I said.

Renee smiled. "You're a good kid," she said. "I wasn't expecting you to come."

"I almost didn't," I admitted.

"Well, now ya know we don't bite," she teased. I knew what she was getting at, but it wasn't their color that made me nervous. It was their religion. A religion that used to be mine and one that I wanted back. I had tried to convince myself that if Cross of Calvary didn't want me, then I should just tell them to go screw themselves and be done with it. But that wouldn't change anything, especially the emptiness I'd been feeling for so long. I looked at Renee. "That's not what I meant," I said. "You know what they put me through."

She patted my hand that was sliding down the smooth wooden pew as we made our way into the center of the aisle. "Of course I do, baby. But don't be thinking on that here. Just enjoy the service."

I sat down next to Mariama and Renee. *Sure, I'll enjoy the service,* I thought. *I'll listen to the upbeat music and the sermon, pray and sing a little, and I'll leave feeling a whole lot better, like a load has been lifted from me. But it won't be long before the doubt and the anger will creep back in, and I'll need to find a new church where no one knows me to get my next spiritual fix.*

Renee turned her head just as the choir appeared at the back of the church. I looked over and saw them in their long white robes. The piano got louder and the choir began to sing at the top of their lungs. They clapped their hands to the beat, practically dancing down the center aisle of the church. The congregation jumped to their feet, clapping and singing along. It took me a second to figure out what was going on, but I eventually got up too. I felt so square next to these people whose bodies moved effortlessly with the music. I stood there awkwardly, clapping my hands like a machine. Mariama looked up at me and giggled.

"I've never done this before," I said.

"It's easy," she said and started dancing, but I could barely hear her over the singing and the clapping. I closed my eyes. There was something about this place; so different from anything I'd ever experienced before. It filled me up, even that pit of emptiness. I felt bad for all those people at Calvary who would never know this feeling because like Luke, they refused to try. They clung to their rules, too scared to let anyone show them that in everything, there is always an exception to the rule.

CHAPTER 15

At work on Tuesday, I was over ten minutes late, but the new supervisor assigned me to register three without noticing the time. I didn't see Jeb or Renee anywhere, so I raced to my register before they appeared out of nowhere and busted me. I scanned the front end for Tina, but there was so sign of her or Tobey either.

It only took a few seconds for people to realize that I was open and for a line to form. A long one. As I took care of one customer, another one entered the back of the line, and it went on like this for most of the shift. I had my head down, running items through the scanner, but I saw Jeb coming toward me out of the corner of my eye. He stopped at the end of my belt with that usual look of superiority spread across his stupid face.

"Turn your light off. You're closed."

"But I have customers."

"No you don't. You're closed. Shut your light off and come with me." I did what I was told and turned off my light. I finished the order I was working on and followed behind Jeb. I could hear the customers in my line complaining and cursing.

I knew what was about to happen, but I kept telling myself I was wrong. I sat down in a plastic chair across from Jeb's desk in his cramped office. I hadn't been in there since the day I filled out my paperwork.

"Simon," he started. Jeb pulled out a piece of paper and placed it in front of me on his desk. "Simon, I'm terminating your employment at the Stop 'n Save. You'll be paid for hours worked, and I need you to sign at the bottom of this page saying you understand what I'm telling you."

I could tell Jeb was enjoying every minute of this. There was nothing I could do about it, but still, I couldn't just let it go. "What am I being fired for?" I asked.

"Tardiness," he replied. "Now sign the page." He tossed a pen onto the desk.

"I have no write-ups for tardiness."

Jeb groaned. "I don't need write-ups, Simon. I have your time card reports. You've been late almost every day for the last month. You were late today. Renee should have written you up weeks ago and believe me, I will be speaking to her about it."

"Fine," I said, trying to hold it together. I picked up the pen and signed the bottom of the paper without even reading it. I stood up. "So what now?"

Jeb started sorting through papers on his desk. He had already moved on. "Clock out and empty your locker," he replied, without looking up. "If you leave quietly, I won't get security involved. Your last paycheck will be mailed to you in a week."

I turned and left, making it a point to slam his office door behind me as hard as I could. Angry tears burned in my eyes, but I held them in. I went straight to the back where I clocked out and threw my time card into the trash. I emptied my locker into a Stop 'n Save bag. I stood there staring at it as panic began to set in. What was I going to do?

I could hear the locker room door open and close. I turned around and saw Tobey walk in.

"Hey," I said. "Where you been?"

"Don't talk to me, Peters," he mumbled and went straight to his locker, where he began emptying everything inside into a knapsack.

"What happened?"

"What does it look like? I got fired!" He slammed shut the locker door and zipped up the bag.

I didn't think it was possible, so I started blurting things out like an idiot. "What! They fired you too? Jeb would never get rid of you! You're perfect!"

"Well, he did, Simon."

"What? He must have given you a reason."

"Cutbacks," he said. "But you know, I think if I hadn't hung out with you I might not have been the one he cut."

"Tobey?" I pleaded. "What do you mean? What did Jeb say?"

"He told me if I wanted to get anywhere in life, I shouldn't be friends with someone like you." Tobey threw his bag over his shoulder. "Ya know, Simon, you're not the only one who really needed this job."

He stormed out of the locker room, and I let him go. He was angry and he'd get over it. I just hoped that what he told me wasn't true. I wondered if Tina and Monique had been fired too. I picked up my grocery bag and walked to the front end.

Jeb was waiting outside the doors between the toy section and the back hall where the locker rooms were. I guess he didn't trust me to leave quietly. "Don't worry, I'm leaving," I mumbled.

"Oh, I know, but since I just had to escort Tina Kingfisher off the property kicking and screaming, I thought I'd better check on you."

I whirled around, knocking some stuffed animals off the shelves with my grocery bag. "Are you firing everyone today?"

"Walk, Mr. Peters." He gave me a little push. I could see why I had it coming but not Tina and definitely not Tobey.

"Let me guess, cutbacks?"

Jeb didn't answer.

I dashed past the line of cashiers, and no one seemed to notice me leaving or even bothered to look up. It didn't surprise me. People were replaced as quickly around here as the lightbulbs. As we approached the supervisor's desk, I saw Renee standing there. She looked upset and was about to say something, but Jeb cut her off.

"Do you have any idea what yer doin'? Not a single write-up for any of 'em? These kids are running around doing whatever the Hell they want on company time." He shook his head. "I knew I shouldn't trust a nigger woman to get anything done right."

For a few seconds it was like all of the air had been sucked out of this huge warehouse. I couldn't believe what I'd just heard.

"Jeb?" I said.

Jeb turned, but rather than a look of concern, he had

an obnoxious sneer across his face. It didn't take long to figure out why. There hadn't been anyone but me and Renee who had heard what he'd just said. It would be our word against his.

"Get out," he said. "You don't work here anymore." Jeb walked away and disappeared behind a display in electronics.

I went up to Renee and put my hand on her shoulder. "You've got to report him," I begged. "Maybe they'll believe you and get rid of him."

"Maybe," she said quietly. "But there'll be others. There always are."

CHAPTER 16

I walked home from the Stop 'n Save in a strange sort of haze, as if I were high or something. After losing my parents and then Stephen, I realized that for the most part, life is just a bunch of events that may seem really amazing or terrible at the time, but are all-in-all pretty forgettable. But like losing the people I loved, this wasn't one of those moments. I was out of job, which meant I had no money, which meant only one thing . . . I was screwed.

Inside the house, Luke was passed out on the couch in front of the TV. I went straight to our bedroom to check on Jude. He was the only reason I'd come inside and hadn't gone straight to find Tina. He was completely covered by the bedsheets and all you could see in the dark was this blue lump gently rising up and down as he breathed. I wanted to wake him up and tell him what had happened. Sometimes I wished that I could talk to him about my problems the way other twin brothers did. But there was nothing Jude could do about me losing my job, and so there was no reason to wake him up and get him all upset. I left the room and stood outside Paul's door, where I could hear his heavy breathing. Confident he was asleep, I went back downstairs.

In the kitchen, there was a piece of scrap wood Dad had nailed to the wall with hooks on it for our car keys. Normally, the Captain would kill anyone who took his truck without asking but it was the middle of the night, and I was betting that I could get back before he woke up.

When I turned the key in the ignition, Paul's radio came blasting on. I fumbled for the button and turned the stupid thing off before it blew my cover. Knowing Paul, he'd have no problem turning me over to the cops for grand theft auto.

Even with no traffic, it took a few minutes to get to the Toucan because it was so far out in the sticks. There were dozens of cars and trucks parked all over the lawn and on the field out front. The porch of the Toucan was lit with naked lightbulbs covered in old spider webs. I saw a lot of guys from the store sitting on the plastic lawn chairs and the benches, which were just wooden slabs nailed to the side of the building. None of the men were talking. Mostly they were hunched over their seats, drinking their beers or whatever was in their glasses . . . just thinking. They weren't there to get drunk and they definitely weren't there to have a good time.

Inside the bar, the air was thick and wet from no AC. Without the jukebox playing, all you could hear were pieces of scattered conversations. Every seat at the bar was taken, and the grizzly looking bartender was staying pretty busy. I scanned the faces, looking for Tina. I didn't see her, but I knew without a doubt that she would be here. The bar was shaped like a U against one wall of the building. I walked around it to the other side and didn't see her there either. *I hope she's just in the bathroom,* I thought to myself.

I sat down at a small table made out of a tree trunk and covered with empty Bud Light bottles. I fiddled with one of them, pulling off the label and rolling the soggy pieces of paper into clumps. I turned around in my seat so I could keep an eye on the door to the girls' bathroom. Tina was in there. I knew it. I just hoped she wasn't puking.

I sat sulking as the bar got steadily busier. It was depressing how little Jeb cared about the people who worked at the Stop 'n Save and how replaceable we all were. For every one of us Jeb fired, there were three high school kids who wanted after-school jobs.

I was about ready to go into the bathroom and look for Tina myself when the door to the girls' room finally swung open and a prostitute in a sparkly blue miniskirt came out. She started putting the moves on the Hubbard brothers who were drinking with a group of friends by the cigarette machine. The hooker's young body didn't seem to match her sagging face, which looked worn out from drugs or maybe just from life. The Hubbard boys weren't paying her much attention so she pulled away from their table and started looking around for a potential customer. I got up and walked over to where she was standing next to the cigarette machine. A few feet away she locked eyes on me like I was the grand prize-winning hog at the county fair.

"Hey, handsome," she said with a smile. "How's your night goin'?"

"Fine, thanks," I answered. "What's your name?"

"Sephora," she said in a sultry voice as she flipped back her streaky blond hair.

"No," I said. "You're getting the wrong idea here. What's your *real* name? I need your help to find my friend. I think she's in the ladies' bathroom."

She gave me a funny look. "Well, when most men come to me for help it costs them, if you know what I mean."

"But what if she's not in there?" I asked.

"Life's risky, baby, and my services are nonrefundable."

"How much then?"

"Well, I can't see this taking too long, so I'll settle for thirty."

"How about you give a guy a break and help him out for twenty?" This Sephora chick was starting to get on my nerves.

"Fine." She put out her hand. I reached into my wallet for the last twenty-dollar bill I had. I wondered what everyone behind us was thinking. I'm pretty sure most of them knew I wasn't the ladies' type.

"You can call me Marie," she said. "What ya need?"

"I'm looking for a friend of mine named Tina," I said. "She hangs out here all the time. She's got long black hair and she's my age. Did you see anyone like that in there?"

"Ya, I mighta seen her. There was a girl with dark hair sitting on the ground next to one of the toilets. The door to the booth was wide open. Whoever she is, she's drunk off her ass."

"Well, if it's her, I need to get her out of there. Can you go back in and check?"

"Sure, why not," she said and started walking toward

the bathrooms. I followed behind her, and as she pushed open the door, she turned to look at me. "So who do I tell her's lookin' for her? How do I know you're not some crazy rapist or something?"

"Just tell her Simon's waiting for her."

"Fine, but if she don't want to see you, then I'm through. I'm not gettin' involved in no domestic dispute." Marie disappeared behind the door. I could hear her high heels clicking on the concrete floor and then voices, but I couldn't make out what they were saying. I waited outside for ten minutes. What was taking so long? I opened the door a crack.

"Marie, is she in there?" I whispered. I could hear the click-clack of her heels again. She came over to the door.

"Ya, it's yer girl and she wants to see you, but I can't get her out of here by myself, so just get in here fast and help me."

She stepped back so I could slip inside. I'd never been inside a girls' bathroom before. It didn't look that much different from the guys'. I followed Marie to the last of the three stalls. Tina was sitting on the floor with her head tilted back against the wall.

"Hey, Simon," she mumbled. "I don't feel so good."

I stepped over her legs so I could get inside the tiny stall. "Well, I'm not surprised," I said. "You've done a real number on yourself, T."

I reached under her arms and pulled her off the floor, using the wall to help carry some of her weight. She put her arm over my shoulder and tried to hold herself up. She couldn't, so I put one arm around her waist and did it for her. Marie wasn't much help in her miniskirt and heels.

She just held Tina's other hand as we got Tina out of the bathroom.

"Don't worry, sugar," she said. "You just need to sleep it off."

The three of us must have been a real sight: a queer and a hooker carrying a drunk girl out of a dive bar in the middle of nowhere. I looked over at Marie and for a second we both smiled. She must have been thinking the same thing. As we passed the bar, I asked the bartender if Tina owed them anything.

"Nah," he said. "Her uncle takes care of it anyways. Just make sure she gets home all right or old Stone'll kill me."

"She'll be fine," I replied. "No thanks to you." I thought there was an unspoken rule that you cut people off once they started puking.

Marie held open the door, and I got Tina outside into the muggy night. I instantly started sweating. The challenging part was getting her down the porch steps. Marie jumped in and held her other arm. I was afraid she was going to trip in those ridiculous shoes and take us all down with her.

"Marie, you're gonna have to help me with the keys," I said, after realizing that there was no way I could support Tina with only one arm. "They're in my left pocket."

Marie didn't think twice about shoving her hand into my pocket and reaching around for the keys. She gave me another sultry look. "Told ya you'd get your money's worth."

"Very funny," I said sarcastically.

I got Tina over to Paul's truck, and Marie opened the

passenger door for me. I never realized how tall trucks are until I had to lift Tina into one. I got her buckled in and closed the door. Her head fell against the window. She was practically asleep now.

"Thanks," I said to Marie. "I won't take up any more of your time."

"Don't worry about it," she replied. "Listen, she told me while I was sittin' with her in the can that she just got fired. Is that true?"

I leaned against the truck to catch my breath. "Yeah, we both did," I answered. "Just one of those days, ya know?"

Marie smiled. "Do I know? Honey, I could write the fuckin' book." She reached into her tight tank top and pulled a bill out of her bra. She handed it to me. It was the twenty bucks I'd given her earlier. At first I tried to give it back, figuring she needed it even more than I did.

"Nah," she said. "You keep it. I really didn't do much anyways." Her lips curled into a smile. "But don't be gettin' any ideas now. I wouldn't do this for just any old john."

"Thanks, Marie," I said. "Take care of yourself, all right?"

"You too," she said. She started walking back toward the bar, her heels sinking into the damp grass. "Now get outta here," she called. "This is no place for a nice kid like you."

I walked around to the other side of the truck and climbed into the driver's seat. Tina let out a moan and shifted in her seat when I started up the engine. It felt like a really long time before I got off the bumpy dirt road and onto the highway. The only other car in sight was a wood-paneled station wagon. It crept up beside us and then moved into our lane.

I looked over at Tina. She was resting against the door with her right arm sprawled over the window frame, so drunk she didn't realize she was drooling all over it. The station wagon drifted off to the left in the direction of Baton Rouge. There was nothing in front of us but darkness and nothing keeping me from driving full speed into the ditch, except the fear of not knowing where my decisions would send me.

CHAPTER 17

I slept until almost noon the next day, which I hadn't done in years. I couldn't face the world and all the questions I didn't have answers to.

Jude was sitting on the edge of my bed looking at me. He was dressed and his hair was neatly combed. I sat up and rubbed my eyes so I could see clearly.

"Hey," I said groggily. "You okay? Did somebody get you breakfast?"

He nodded. "I have something to show you," he signed. He reached behind his back and picked something off the bed. He pulled it around and placed it in front of me—a small purple fig. His face broke into a huge smile. "From our tree."

I picked up the tiny fruit. It was soft to the touch, but its flesh was hard, definitely not ripe.

"It will continue to ripen," signed Jude, reading my mind.

I smiled at him. I knew he was looking for a reaction. "Well, this *is* exciting," I said. "Congratulations."

"It wasn't me," he signed. "It just knew it was the right time."

I handed the fig back to Jude who cradled it in his hands like a baby. I pushed the sheet to the end of my bed. "Time to get this over with," I murmured. Jude was all smiles and lost in his own little world, so I didn't disturb him. *Let him be happy,* I thought. *He will be one less thing I'll have to worry about today.* Jude followed me down the stairs and into the living room. Luke should have been at work by now, but instead he was sitting on the couch staring out the window.

"Hey," I said. He looked up.

"Hey, Paul just called. He heard some rumor that you got fired."

I rolled my eyes. Paul hadn't heard some rumor I'd been fired. He'd just heard there'd been layoffs at the store and assumed his no-good brother was one of them. "Yeah, me and a bunch of other people. Tina too. So why aren't you at work?" I asked him.

"I called off," he answered. "I thought I should stay home with you and Jude. Maybe start acting like a big brother for a change." He looked at me like he was asking for my forgiveness. Probably for all the times he'd joked around and acted like nothing mattered so he wouldn't have to deal with real life.

"Thanks," I said.

Jude sat down next to Luke on the couch and showed him the tiny fig. "Good job, little buddy," he said. "You're a regular Farmer Brown." Luke didn't seem his normal self at all.

"Simon," he said. "I've got something I need to tell you."

Oh shit, I thought. *That's never good.* I remembered the somber operating room doctor walking slowly into the waiting room after the car accident. "Boys, there's something I need to tell you . . ."

"Go ahead," I said, bracing myself.

He cleared his throat and by the way he didn't look directly at me, I knew that what he was about to say wasn't going to be easy. "You know how I said that I turned down all those schools after Mom and Dad died?" I nodded. "Well, that's not exactly what I did. I just deferred my acceptance for a year so I could stay here with you guys and help out. And, I mean, I had no idea you were gonna lose your job or anything, so last week I just went ahead and accepted for the fall semester. I start in August."

"*Last* week?" I stammered.

"I was gonna tell you sooner, but I was pissed off at Paul."

"What's that got to do with me?" I snapped. I couldn't believe he hadn't told me that he was even *thinking* about going back to school.

Jude shook Luke's arm so he would look at him. "Where are you going?" he signed.

"To Baton Rouge, little buddy," he answered quickly. He turned back to me. "Simon, I get why you're angry, but—"

"*No*, you don't!" I yelled. "This changes everything! I can't do this by myself, Luke, not anymore. There's *no* way!"

Jude had wrapped his arms around himself and was swaying gently. He was so scared he didn't realize he was squishing his precious fig. Luke pried Jude's hands away from his body. "You don't need to be here for this, little buddy," he said. "Why don't you . . . um, get us all some Kool-Aid, okay?"

Jude got up, his arms still wrapped tightly around his body, and stumbled past me into the kitchen.

"Why'd you have to upset him?" I spat. "Couldn't you see how happy he was? Or do you have to be the Captain now and make everybody miserable?" I didn't want to yell at Luke. I loved him. I *needed* him. But I was losing him too, and I didn't know what to do. I felt like everything was slipping away.

"I'm *sorry*," he said. "Do you honestly think I would have accepted if I had known you were gonna get fired?"

I was finding it hard to breathe, like the time Luke pushed me off the deck onto an exposed nail that shot clear through my foot. I leaned forward with my hands on my legs and lowered my head. I had never been so scared in my entire life. I was even too scared to cry. A million horrible thoughts started whizzing through my mind. How would I take care of Jude? Where would we live? Then I thought about Stephen and realized if I had no place for him to go, he'd be stuck at that Waverley Christian Center.

"Simon? Come on, man, talk to me," he pleaded.

I slowly raised my head. "I really don't know, Luke," I replied. He seemed surprised. Maybe even hurt. Did he just assume that I thought he would always love me, stick by me because he was my brother? Had Paul not proven again and again this wasn't the case?

"I dunno what to do," said Luke. "I *am* sorry. If you don't want me to go, I won't go."

He looked like he meant it, but I knew I was in a lose-lose situation. If he left, I would have no help taking care of Jude. If he stayed, I'd feel guilty for screwing up another person's life. "No, you have to go," I said. "But can you at least watch Jude for me today while I try and get my own shit together?"

"Of course!" He shot up in his seat. "I got Jude. You go do what you gotta do. You're smart, little bro. You'll figure something out before August."

"Thanks," I mumbled and headed for the door. I had to get out of the house. I didn't even think I could keep my cool long enough to say good-bye to Jude. *You'll figure something out?* Really? For a smart guy, Luke was so clueless sometimes.

The Captain's truck was gone. No escape route there. And I couldn't bring myself to go back inside and ask for Luke's keys. I would have to walk to the highway and hitch a ride to the trailer park. I needed to talk to Tina—*sober.*

I wasn't running, but I wasn't walking either. Completely absorbed in my own thoughts, I didn't see Stan Rafferty standing at the corner of our street and Byrne Avenue.

"Hey," he said.

I came out of my daze and looked at him. *No insult,* I thought. *No "queer." No "fairy." What does he want?*

"I heard about the shit that went down at the store," he continued.

"Apparently everyone has."

"So, what are you gonna do?" he asked.

Now I was on my guard. Why did he care? "If you wanna know whether I'm leaving town, it's a definite possibility," I snapped. "Would that make you happy, Stanipoo?"

He smiled but stayed perfectly calm, something he never did. Stan wasn't much good at controlling his temper.

"Listen, Peters, I know you and I haven't exactly been *friends*."

"No kidding, Stan," I mumbled.

"But we don't have to be friends to be, well, part-ners . . . colleagues; however you want to put it."

I looked at him, bewildered. Stan Rafferty wanted *me* to work for him. "Ah, no thanks, Stan," I answered quickly and started walking away, but an unanswered question made me stop. Why would Stan want me selling his stuff? He hated me. I turned to face him again. "Why the Hell would you want me to be your 'partner' anyways?" I asked.

He just shrugged. "Well, it's better than you being my liability," he answered. "We both think so. But have it your way, Peters." Stan brushed past me and kept walking toward our houses.

First of all, I didn't think Stan Rafferty knew what big words like "liability" meant, but he had also said "we." Who was he talking about? I kept up my earlier pace until I came to the end of Byrne, where I hopped a small barricade and was just a few feet away from I-10. I stared blankly at the few cars that passed by and then it hit me. Hit me sharply the way Paul's hand had that one morning when he slapped me. *Paul.* Paul didn't trust me, and he definitely didn't trust Jude, so he would have to keep us close. Close enough so that we wouldn't blab to the wrong people about Lydia and the baby, so that we wouldn't expose what he was selling at work, so that we wouldn't destroy his wholesome image that was now just a fading veneer. Love thy enemies. Isn't that what Jesus had done? And Paul was such a good Christian. He would say he had learned from the best.

I walked to the edge of the highway and stuck my thumb into the air. I walked backward, slowly keeping my eyes on the road. A white sedan passed, then a maroon Buick. Fifteen minutes later a silver Tundra approached. The driver saw me and pulled over. I walked up to the side of the truck, and the window rolled down.

"Simon?" asked a familiar voice. I peered into the truck and saw Matt Lebeau. Matt was the weapons-and-firearms expert in the hunting and camping department at the Stop 'n Save.

"You need a ride somewhere, man?" he asked.

"Yeah," I answered. "I'm trying to get to the trailer park on Zion. You headed that way?"

"Yeah," he said. "No problem. Jump in."

"Thanks. My brothers are at work so I couldn't bum a ride." I climbed into the passenger seat.

"Don't mention it. Perfect that I just happened to be driving by, huh?"

"Yeah, sure is," I said.

"So, ah, did you survive the purge yesterday?" he asked. Now I was confused. "Purge?"

"Thirty people rifted in one day. Cutbacks is the excuse they gave me. Economy's bad and there isn't enough demand for a dedicated weapons expert. I told them they were gonna get somebody killed."

Thirty people, I thought. Shit, Jeb really was cleaning house. I wondered what beef he had with a decent guy like Matt Lebeau. "Jeb said I was late too much," I replied. "And I can't really argue with him on that one."

"Sorry, man," he said. "But, hey, you wanna know what I'm gonna do?" I did, so I nodded. "I'm gonna join the police force. Become a state trooper," he declared proudly. "I always thought it was my calling, and now I have no more excuses. I plan on getting things started this afternoon."

I was impressed. Matt had been unemployed less than twenty-four hours, and he already had a plan. He was going to follow his dream. I tried to think of my own dreams. It took a while. Living with Stephen and Jude somewhere far away from this place. Having a decent job with a decent boss. Had I let those dreams slip away almost to the point that I could barely remember them? It hurt too much to think about how far away they were from anything close to reality.

CHAPTER 18

Matt let me out at the entrance to the trailer park. He tapped his horn as he pulled back onto Zion Road. I walked down the row of mobile homes and saw a group of kids playing outside. Their moms and dads were sitting on their porches, talking as they kept half an eye on them. I smiled and walked past them, wishing I was a kid again.

I could see Tina's light blue double-wide coming up on the right. I thought of Matt Lebeau and his plans to go back to school to become a state trooper. That was *exactly* how Tina needed to approach this whole thing. I could also picture Tina with a guy like Luke. He might have been a real jerk for bailing on me, but I still knew he was an upgrade from Tina's other boyfriends. She had a high school degree and plenty of work experience; she just needed someone to push her in the right direction. Maybe knowing that Luke was going to college would convince her to apply to LSU.

I walked up onto the little porch and knocked on the door. I was surprised when Tina's sister, Angie, opened it. She looked at me with these huge sad eyes. "I am really sorry, Simon," she said. "Tina called this morning and told us what happened yesterday. But at least you two aren't the only ones," she added quickly. "I hear they had to let go a bunch of people because of the economy."

"Yup, it was kind of a bloodshed over there," I said. "But thanks. I'll be fine. How's our girl?"

"Hurtin' pretty bad. She'll be glad to see you. Come on in." I walked into the tiny living room. "She's stopped throwing up, at least, thank God."

Tina was sitting on the couch wrapped in a blanket and looking even paler than normal. I was about to say something to her when a little old lady scurried into the living room. In her cotton floral dress and white cardigan, Tina's grandmother looked like a character from a Norman Rockwell painting. That is until she flashed a look of death at Tina and then at me. Without a word, she picked up her purse from the table next to the door and left the trailer.

Angie looked at me expectantly. "Simon, I, ah, have to go pick up Chris from work and as you can see our grandma's got plans. Could you . . . maybe . . ." She looked over at Tina. I didn't let her finish.

"Don't worry. I'll make sure she doesn't puke all over your grandmother's couch."

Angie let out a short laugh. "Thanks. I won't be long." She walked over to Tina, said a few words, and then turned, grabbing her bag off the coffee table before dashing out the door.

I went and sat next to my patient on the couch. "Hey, albino girl," I joked. "Feelin' a little under the weather, huh?"

She turned her head to look at me and despite feeling

miserable, she smiled. "Simon," she whispered. Her voice was hoarse, but she sounded happy to see me.

"You okay?" I asked.

"I'm hungover, but I'll be fine . . . I guess." She rested her head on my shoulder and started slinking her thin fingers through my hair.

"Yeah, I know what you mean."

We said nothing for a little while. Tina's fingers gently massaged my scalp, and it felt good. She was the first to break the silence.

"Truthfully, I feel like shit. Jeb's fucked up all those people's lives."

"That's the hangover, T." I laughed. "It'll wear off, I promise."

"You *know* what I mean," she snapped. "He talked to me like I was a two-year-old with no brains."

I sighed, not too sure that I was going to get anywhere with her in this condition. She just needed to be miserable for a while; at least until the headache and nausea wore off.

"I'm worried about all those people," she said.

"Don't be," I replied. "You need to think about yourself and what you're gonna do. Man, T, do all girls worry as much as you do?"

"You're the first one I've met who worried more," she said with a smug grin.

"That was low."

She moved her slender fingers down to my earlobe and started massaging it. "Sorry," she said, but she was still smiling.

"The only person I'm really worried about is Tobey," I admitted. "Besides you, of course. I mean the kid's life was that store."

Tina groaned. "They got him too!"

"I'll check on him today," I said. "I'll make sure he's hangin' in there." I decided not to tell her that Tobey believed I was responsible for him getting rifted.

Tina nestled closer.

"You realize that there's only one logical thing for us to do," I said to change the subject.

"What?" she asked.

"Remember when we were talking about me getting my GED and you going to college and we made a sort of pact?"

"*Simon,*" she whined. "Not that again."

"Come on, T, you promised." I was lying through my teeth as I had no intentions of getting my GED anytime soon. I hated to admit it, but what I needed was for someone else to take care of her for a while so I could get my own shit together. If she were at college where she could talk to counselors and professors and had friends like Luke who'd bail her out of messy parties, I knew she'd be okay without me.

"All right, all right," she allowed. "I'll *think* about it."

"What's there to think about? What else are you gonna do? Besides, that's what everyone else is doing."

"Whadya mean everyone else is? Who else?" she asked.

"Matt Leabeau. He gave me a ride, and he's going to get training to become a state trooper."

"Why did Matt Lebeau drive you here?" Tina interrupted.

"Long story, don't worry about it. So, yeah, there's Matt Lebeau and Luke also." I waited anxiously, hoping that the mention of Luke would create a reaction. It did, and much more quickly than I'd expected. She pushed her upper body off the couch with her one arm and looked me. I couldn't read her face right away. Was it surprise? No, the way her forehead wrinkled and her tiny, delicate lips gaped open, she was panicking.

"Where's Luke going?" she blurted.

I couldn't help but smile. "Relax," I said, pushing her back against the small frilly pillow she had been lying on. "He's decided to finally go to premed. He leaves for Baton Rouge in August."

"B-b-but what about you and Jude?" she asked.

Great, I thought. Maybe she was more concerned about how his leaving would affect me and not her. "We'll be fine, T," I lied. "Luke's been doing his own thing for a while anyways, and this is something he needs to do. Just like how becoming a teacher is something *you* need to do, so stop giving me a hard time."

"We should all go together," she declared. "Get a place in Baton Rouge."

I wanted to consider her idea. It sounded so simple and perfect. But there was one person who needed to be added into the puzzle, and his placement was not as clear as the others. Where did Stephen fit into my life? Did he fit at all now, or had too much changed?

"Tina," I began, "that's a nice idea and all, but I kind of think Luke needs a break from Jude, and besides, you two would be good together, even just as friends."

"Stop it!" she shouted and sat up again, glaring at me

with those ferocious black eyes of hers. "Stop trying to take care of everybody else and start taking care of yourself for a change!"

I didn't know how to explain to her that that was exactly what I was trying to do. "Please just call him, T," I pleaded. "He's home now and you can ask him about those application and scholarship questions you had."

"*Simon*, you're not listening to me!"

"Please, Tina!" I was begging her now. "I *am* listening to you, but you don't get it. I need you to *let* me start taking care of myself." At that moment, she finally understood. I was terrified I had hurt her feelings. That she would think I was trying to get rid of her. She continued looking at me, but her face had softened. No, I realized, I hadn't hurt her feelings at all. I had given her a free pass, and she had given me one. Neither one of us was bound any longer to take care of the other. Tina wanted to get away and go to college. Maybe she always had. And now she could.

"Okay," she said. "I'll call him. We'll figure something out."

"Thanks," I replied. "I feel better. You know Luke needs someone. He can only microwave things, and I think he might starve to death in Baton Rouge."

This made her smile. "Note taken. So, then, what *are* you gonna do?"

"I don't really know," I admitted. "The Captain'll marry Lydia soon and move out, so I guess we'll sell the house and split whatever's left after the mortgage is paid *if* there is anything left."

"Where will you go?"

I didn't have to think very long. "To get Stephen," I said. "See if we can actually make this work."

"I've seen how he looks at you," she said. "I know you can."

I hoped she was right. "Well, you look like you're feeling better," I said. I didn't want to talk about the future anymore.

"I think a little bit."

"Do you want some water?" I asked.

"Thanks, that would be great."

I went into her tiny kitchen and searched through a few cabinets before I found a glass. I cracked a few ice cubes out of a tray and dropped them in. I filled the glass with cold water and went back into the living room.

"I hope I can keep this down," she said.

"You and me both. I promised your sister I wouldn't let you make a mess of your grandma's couch."

She giggled. "Whatever. This thing has been drowned in that spray-on fabric protector. Not even I could harm it." Tina started sipping on her water. I sat down next to her. We sat together like that for a little while, not saying too much. She asked how Jude took the news about Luke leaving for school.

"I doubt he understands," I answered. "But I dunno. I don't give him enough credit sometimes. He knows a lot more than people think . . . about everything."

When Angie and Chris arrived back a few minutes later, they had a Winn-Dixie bag with vitamin water and soup for Tina. Angie went into the kitchen, and I followed her.

"You think she could stomach some of this?" Angie asked, holding up a can of tomato soup.

"Maybe a little, but make it with water, not milk, just in case."

"Good call," she said and searched around for a can opener. "Thanks for keepin' her company while I was out."

"Don't mention it. You know, Tina's like a sister to me."

"Yeah, well you've been around more often when she needed help than I have."

"Don't beat yourself up," I said. "You found a life for yourself and so will Tina. Trust me, I'm all over it."

"Thanks," she said. "I'm glad she has you and, uh, I'll be the deadbeat sister who makes sure she eats." Angie whisked a can of water into the lump of red goo. We both stood there staring at the pot while the soup heated up. "You know I saw Lydia yesterday at work. She gave me an invitation to the wedding. It was really pretty. Have you seen it yet?"

My one hand gripped the counter. *No*, I hadn't seen any invitations. I didn't even know they'd set a date. "Um, yeah, I mean they're kind of girlie, but it's her wedding, so whatever." I hoped that sounded convincing.

Angie smiled. "Yeah, Lydia loves frilly things. I just can't believe it's on August Sixth. Ya know, that's in, what, two weeks?"

I wasn't sure if I could hide my shock. *Two* weeks? How did I not know that my brother was getting married in two weeks? "I know, it's crazy," I answered. "But I mean, we were expecting a shotgun wedding anyways. Paul's freaking out about this baby, the timing of it, I mean."

Angie pulled the pot off the stove and poured some of

the soup into a bowl. "I don't know why he's hiding it," she said, as she pulled a spoon out of a drawer.

"*I* do."

She looked up at me. "Oh, right, you religious types."

I almost laughed. It had been awhile since I'd considered myself a "religious type" and even longer since I was considered one by anybody else. "It just looks bad," I said. I thought of Mr. and Mrs. Lévesques' disapproving glares and Pastor Ted's fire-and-brimstone sermons. If I were Paul, I'd hide a pregnancy out of wedlock from them too. "Anyways, he's made up his mind."

Angie shrugged and picked up the bowl of soup to take to Tina. "Coming?" I nodded and followed her.

Chris was flipping through the channels on the TV. Tina accepted the soup from Angie but sipped it very slowly.

"Aren't you going to sit down?" Chris asked, after I'd been standing next to the TV for about five minutes, watching Tina eat.

"Oh, uh, no, I should probably get going. I need to drop by Tobey's place and check on him." I walked over to Tina and gave her a kiss on the head. "Are you gonna be fine now?"

"Yeah," she answered. "Don't worry about me. I'll call Luke a little later. I promise."

"Good." I turned to Angie and Chris to say good-bye.

"Wait, how did you get here?" Angie asked. "I didn't see a car outside."

"Well, actually, I hitchhiked over," I answered. "Long story."

Angie's eyes widened. "You *hitchhiked*? Is that how you were planning on getting back?"

I just shrugged. "Yeah, I guess."

She shook her head. "You could have just *asked*." She sounded a little irritated.

"You want me to drive him?" Chris asked.

"No, I'll take him." I was about to argue when Angie pointed her finger at me like she wasn't going to have any of it. "Seriously, it's the least I can do." She looked over at Tina and smiled. "For all the times you took care of this walking disaster." Tina made a face at her sister.

I said good-bye to Chris and Tina and trailed after Angie to her car.

"Thanks," I said as I got into the passenger side. "You might be saving my life from some psychopath who likes to pick off hitchhikers."

She laughed. "Don't mention it. So where to?"

CHAPTER 19

We pulled off the gravel driveway and drove slowly past the children to Zion Road. "My friend Tobey lives at the Magnolia Apartments."

Angie scrunched her nose. "*That* dump?"

"Unfortunately."

"Poor kid. Serious white trash at that place." She nodded in the direction of the now fading trailer park. "And I would know."

The trailer park had a bad reputation, which was undeserved, but everything bad I heard about the Magnolia Apartments was always true. The place was a popular hangout for junkies, dealers, and pimps. It also wouldn't have surprised me if that one building had a higher number of domestic disturbances per year than the three surrounding parishes combined.

The Magnolia Apartments were in a three-story, yellowing concrete building on the outskirts of town, which is exactly where they belonged. The building was elevated to make room for parking underneath. Angie pulled over and dropped me off on the curb. After thanking her for about the millionth time, I got out and walked up to a large, metal door that had a keypad above the handle. I didn't know the combination. The only person around was an old black man sitting in a blue-and-white beach chair on a concrete slab next to the door. It must have been too early in the day for the pimps and hos.

"I'm here to see Tobey Hale," I said. The man just nodded and thought on what I had said for about thirty seconds as he stared straight ahead at the passing traffic. I was about to turn to leave when he spewed out a series of numbers. "Two-two-nine-six-eight." He never looked away from the road.

I entered the numbers into the keypad and the door opened. "Thanks," I mumbled and walked inside a foyer that smelled like urine. I didn't trust the elevators, not for a second. There were three of them, and they looked just like the rest of the building, as if they hadn't been touched since the seventies. The door to the middle elevator seemed to be permanently in a half-closed, half-open position. Around the corner was a set of stairs, and I tried my luck with them. I knew from talking to Tobey that he lived on the second floor in apartment twenty-seven. I had never visited him before, even though he had invited me over a few times. Because of taking care of Jude, it had been a cinch to come up with excuses. I looked around at the institutional white walls and dirty plastic flooring. I felt like I was back in the rehab center visiting Stephen, and I couldn't help but feel a little guilty. Would it have killed me to have hung out at Tobey's place just once? The poor guy was probably losing his mind in here.

I arrived at number twenty-seven and knocked on the

white metal door. Unlike my visit to Tina, who I knew would be bedridden from a hangover, I had no idea if Tobey would be home. I heard a faint shuffling inside; not much sound could penetrate the ridiculous metal door. I guessed people around the Magnolia Apartments had to worry about flying bullets. The handle turned, and Tobey appeared in the dark entranceway.

He seems okay, I thought to myself. His eyes weren't bloodshot from crying or anything, but I couldn't be sure so I started spewing an apology. "Tobey, I am *so* sorry. If I had any clue Jeb would have fired you because of me I would have—"

"*Stop*, Simon," he interrupted. There was a strength in his voice that I had never heard before. I stood there, looking at him dumbfounded. "I was a shitty friend," he continued. "So stop apologizing."

"Uh . . . okay," I mumbled like an idiot.

A huge smile broke across his face. "Well, are you coming in or not?"

"Um, sure," I answered and walked into the dark apartment.

There was a grimy beige couch, a TV on a metal stand, and a small four-piece dining set from the Stop 'n Save do-it-yourself furniture department. The builder's special kitchen overlooked the living room, and I assumed that around the corner down a narrow hallway was the bedroom and bathroom.

"Have a seat," he said. "Want a Coke? I have beer too."

"Coke's fine. Thanks." I took a seat on his couch. Tobey had made an effort to work with the boring white walls. A few posters were taped up above the couch and next to the dining room table. He handed me a soda and sat down at the other end of the couch.

"You know, man, I can't believe you're handling this so well," I said as I cracked open the can.

"Yeah, I was about ready to kill you yesterday." Tobey took a chug of his soda. "Sorry about that. It was stupid of me to blame you just because Jeb doesn't like that you're . . . well, you know."

"Oh, I know," I said. "I get it. I would have been pissed if I were you too."

Tobey became very serious. "At first, getting fired hurt almost as bad as when my mom died. Working at the Stop 'n Save allowed me to be independent, so I wouldn't have to go back and live with my dad."

I felt my body stiffen. How did I not know that Tobey's mother was dead too? I didn't know because I had never bothered to ask about his family. I thought Tobey could sense my embarrassment.

"I never wanted to talk about it," he said.

"Doesn't mean I couldn't have asked."

"Don't worry about it. We're cool," he said.

"Have you thought about what you're gonna do?"

"All freakin' day. I've been driving myself crazy. I've got some money saved so I'll be fine for a while. I called my cousin who's a developer, and he said he has some work for me, at least 'til the end of the summer, but I'm like ninety-nine percent positive that Home Depot is opening up in that empty lot where the Plant House used to be."

"Awesome," I said. "Yeah, I heard the rumors about Home Depot too. That would be really good for the town."

"So what about you?" he asked.

"No idea."

"Tina?"

"I'm trying to convince her to go to college," I answered. "Luke's going to LSU in the fall, so I told her to call him and they can like, I dunno, be *smart* together."

"Luke's leaving?" he asked. "How're you gonna take care of Jude by yourself? I mean, it was rough enough when you had a job."

"Um . . . don't exactly know," I mumbled. "Haven't gotten that far yet." I tried to laugh a little, thinking he'd drop the subject.

"Y'all are welcome to stay here," he proposed. "Anytime. I know it ain't a resort or anything, but it's better than being put out on the street."

"Thank you," I said, and I genuinely meant it. Tobey was the first person who had actually offered me help and not just his useless sympathy. "Listen, man, I'd better get going. I left Jude with Luke all morning. Thanks for the Coke." I got up from my seat and walked toward the door. Tobey did the same.

"Sure, no problem, Simon. Thanks for comin' by."

"Don't mention it. I'm glad you're gonna be okay." I walked into the hall and had to shield my eyes from the afternoon sun. He stood leaning against the doorway.

"You're gonna be okay too. Just, uh . . . don't let them change you, Simon. I'm pretty sure we've lost enough already." He turned to go back inside. "See you around."

"See you around, Tobey," I said as he closed the door. I walked down the stairs, out the front entrance, and passed the old man who was still sitting motionless in his beach chair. I had a fifteen mile walk ahead of me back to the house. I thought about Tobey and what he had said to me right before saying good-bye. I had just about come to terms with the fact that I wasn't going to change. I didn't know what was going to happen to me, or to Stephen, but one thing was clear. This time I would fight for him. And I would fight for myself.

CHAPTER 20

I jogged the last half mile to the house. It didn't matter that it was ninety-three out with five hundred percent humidity. I had to get back to Jude. He would be scared and confused that Luke and I had been fighting because we hardly ever fought. I ran through the front door and was greeted by a soothing wave of cold air. I looked down and saw that someone had turned on the big oscillating fan. "Jude!" I called.

"He's outside in the garden," said Luke who was still on the couch watching TV. An empty bottle of beer and a plate with a few crumbs were on the coffee table in front of him. "Oh, and the Captain's here. He wants to talk to you."

"*Great,*" I mumbled.

Luke smiled. "I don't think it's bad. I'm pretty sure it's about the wedding. They've set a date."

"Yeah, so I've heard," I answered. A confused look spread across his face. *Poor guy,* I thought. *He must have thought we were the first to know.* "So have you two made up then?" I asked.

"Of course," he said with a shrug. "We're brothers."

So what does that mean? I wanted to ask him. *What*

does being brothers allow you to do? To threaten, to hurt, to abandon, but always to be forgiven? Where was forgiveness when Paul found out about Stephen and me?

"I'm gonna check on Jude," I said. I walked through the kitchen and back out into the muggy afternoon. Jude was sitting on the grass next to the fig tree. He was in a fetal position, with his arms wrapped tightly around his legs. He looked upset, but he wasn't swaying.

"Hey," I said, as I sat down across from him.

Jude looked up and smiled. He released his legs and signed "Hi" with his now free hands.

"Sorry I took so long. I had to check on some friends."

"Tina?" he asked.

"Yeah, she asked about you." Tina hadn't, but I was sure that if she hadn't been feeling so sick she would have, and besides, I was willing to say anything to make him feel better. I leaned back on my hands and gazed up at the fig tree. I was surprised that some of the long, hand-like leaves were wilting. Hadn't this thing just produced a fruit? Jude must have seen the confusion in my face.

"It's dying," he signed.

"Nah, don't be pessimistic," I said. "It just made a fig. It'll be fine. Maybe it's too hot right now or we need to water it some more."

Jude didn't say anything. He knew something I didn't, but when it came to gardening, I knew next to nothing. "Listen, can we go inside?" I asked. "I can't handle the heat today." Jude nodded, and we both got up. My clothes were sticking to me from jogging home.

"Have you eaten?" I asked. Jude shook his head. "Crap," I mumbled. Jude's eyes widened. "Sorry, it's not you," I added quickly. "It's just Luke is so useless. I can't leave you with anybody."

Jude followed me into the kitchen, and I tried to cheer him up by making him one of his favorites for dinner: grilled cheese sandwiches with slices of tomato and the crusts cut off. Jude sat at the kitchen table, and I gave him some cherry Kool-Aid. I was cutting two sandwiches into little triangles when Paul walked into the kitchen.

"Simon," he said, as though saying my name counted as a greeting.

"Paul," I answered. I handed the plate of sandwich pieces to Jude.

Paul opened his mouth to say something when Jude turned his chair around to face both of us. "Why didn't you tell me you lost your job?" he signed.

I could have killed Luke. Who else would have told him? "Because I didn't want you to get upset," I answered. "I've got this completely under control and besides, you know I wasn't happy there. This change will be good for me. It'll be good for both of us." Jude's expression didn't change. I'm a terrible liar and he knew this better than anyone.

"Jude," said Paul. "Would you mind taking your dinner into the living room and eating with Luke? I need to talk to Simon for a minute."

Jude got up and went into the living room with his dinner. I crossed my arms over my chest and leaned against the counter, waiting for the barrage of disapproval to start. It didn't, though. Paul came closer and stood in front of to me. There was no anger anywhere on his face.

"Simon, what was that?" he asked, gesturing his head

toward the living room where Jude was now eating his sandwich.

"What else could I do?" I asked. "He looked scared. I'm just trying to give him a little hope."

"But it's *false* hope, Simon."

"Is there any other kind?" I shot back.

Paul didn't know what to say after that. I hadn't really meant it. I didn't know what I was saying. I unlocked my arms from my chest and placed my hands behind me on the counter. I stared down at the kitchen floor. It was dirty. I tried to remember when someone, I guess that would have been me, had last washed it. I felt a strong hand bracing my shoulder. Paul was standing over me. Normally, I'd be freaked out when he did that, but not this time. Something about this time was different.

"You can't take care of him, Simon. Not anymore. It's too much." His voice was unusually kind. "You *don't* have this under control."

My jaw locked as I fought back the angry tears, but I was no match for them. I shuddered and the next time I tried to breathe a heavy sob ripped through me. "I failed him," I choked, desperately trying to hold it together. I never allowed myself to be this vulnerable in front of Paul. He always knew how to take advantage of my weaknesses.

He came around in front of me and grasped my other shoulder, gently shaking me. "No you didn't," he said firmly. "This is not your fault. It's gotten too hard for all of us."

I took a deep breath. "I dunno what to do." Paul's hands slid off my shoulders, and suddenly they were wrapped around my back in a hug. I froze with my hands hanging limply at my sides. I tried to think of the last time we had hugged. Not at the funeral. Not in *years*. Had Paul finally forgiven me? I should have known better than to just assume that, but at the same time I didn't care. I had buried how much his rejection had hurt and now all that hurt was swimming up to the surface. I held on to him tightly and let the tears collect on his shirt where I had my face pressed against his shoulder.

"I'm going to make this go away," he said. "You're gonna be fine."

I didn't argue with him or demand to know how he was going to fix this impossible situation. I didn't care. I just wanted to know that, somehow, he would. I pulled back to try and get myself together. I grabbed a dish towel and wiped my face like it was a dinner plate. I felt like a huge burden had been lifted. Paul and I were buddies again, and he wasn't going to let me go through this alone.

"Do you want to know what I *actually* came in here to talk to you about?" he asked with a huge smile on his face.

"Sure," I replied.

He stood back with his hands stretched out. "We set a date!" he shouted triumphantly.

Oh right, the *wedding*. I still didn't like Lydia, but I hadn't seen Paul this happy in forever so I played along. "Awesome! So when do I need to rent the tux?"

"August sixth, but no tux required. All of the grooms-men are going to wear khaki pants, a white shirt, and a different colored tie. I dunno, the tie thing was Lydia's idea. She thinks she can coordinate y'all with her bridesmaids."

"Wait a second," I said. "Did you say *groomsmen*? You want *me* to be in your wedding?" This wouldn't have been strange in most families, but in mine, Paul asking me to be one of his groomsmen was worth calling the local news.

He was smiling from ear to ear. "Sure do, little brother," he said. "You and I are turning over a new leaf. Water under the bridge and all that good stuff."

I couldn't believe it. I'd been waiting to hear those words for I don't know how long. I *had* been forgiven.

"I'd be honored!" I exclaimed.

Paul slapped his hands together. "Excellent. Well, I have a lot more stuff I need to tell you and Luke about, but that can wait; I think you need a night off."

"Got that covered, but thanks."

"Not from the store," he continued, "from Jude. Lydia and I will take him out so you can have some time to yourself."

I couldn't hide my surprise. We'd officially moved on from the local news to CNN. "That would be really great," I replied without even thinking about what I was agreeing to. "But are you guys okay with taking Jude out? I mean, you were ready to kill him the other night."

"Forgotten," Paul replied. "You go have fun and *I* will take care of Jude."

"Okay," I said. "He won't mind."

"Of course not," Paul answered. "Besides, he's too dependent. We need to wean him off you, ya know, get him used to different people."

I didn't know about the "weaning him off" of me part, but I did know that I needed a break so I could think things through. I needed a night to myself, and Paul was giving me that. There were strings attached. There always were with Paul, but I wasn't interested right now in what it might cost me.

"Go on," he said. "Go take a shower. You look like you just ran a marathon or something."

I looked down at my sweat-streaked clothes. "Yeah, and I probably don't smell too good either." Paul scrunched his nose and shook his head.

"Yeah, I'll get right on that," I said, walking past him to the kitchen door. I turned to look at him. "Thanks, Paul. It's really cool you're doing this."

"Ah, don't mention it, little brother." Paul flashed me a reassuring smile and then opened the fridge door to get a beer.

As I passed the living room, I saw Jude sitting silently next to Luke watching *M*A*S*H* reruns. His plate was empty. "I'm going upstairs to take a shower," I said.

Jude looked up at me with a crazy grin on his face. "Good!" he signed.

"You know you could have *told* me I reeked!"

Jude started laughing his silent laugh, with his mouth wide open and his shoulders bobbing up and down. "I won't be long." I headed up the stairs, trying to ignore the rumblings of guilt about not telling Jude I was handing him over to the Captain for the night. I ran a cold shower, and as I stood under the icy water, I tried to organize my thoughts. Paul had said he was going to "make this go away," but I didn't know what that meant. Knowing Paul, he was probably going to help me find another job and then I'd be on my own, but that was fine with me. I had no problem with Paul selling the house and moving somewhere else with Lydia. As long as I had a job that could pay the bills, I could find a cheap place for Jude and me to live. The Magnolia Apartments weren't *that* bad. Renting a place there would only be temporary anyways. Jude would understand. I would get Stephen out

of that Hellhole, and then he'd see I was serious about us being together. Stephen was smart. He'd find a job, and then we'd get a nicer place with a yard for Jude. Stephen could work days and I'd take the night shift again so Jude wouldn't be alone. I'd feel bad asking Stephen to look after Jude at night, but I wouldn't have a choice. A relationship with me was a package deal.

We would have to leave town. There was no doubt about that. Stephen would never set foot in this place again, and who could blame him? Everything would remind him of his family, and to them he was as good as dead.

I washed myself and my hair a bunch of times to make sure I got rid of the sweat smell. I must have been in the shower a long time, since the skin on my fingers had puckered. I dried off and put on clean clothes. I felt like a new man. I headed back downstairs and saw Luke sprawled across the couch.

"Where's Jude?" I asked.

Luke turned to look at me and then shifted himself around so that he was sitting upright. "Weirdest thing, little bro," he said. "*Paul* took him out. They're going to pick up Lydia from the store and go bowling or something. He said he talked to you about it."

My heart sank. "*Bowling!*" I moaned. "Jude hates loud noises. He cries when I vacuum!"

"Well, Paul wasn't sure they'd go bowling. They may just take him to the park."

"I hope so. Paul means well but he really doesn't know anything about Jude."

"Means well?" Luke asked. "Sounds like you two have made up."

"Seems so. Paul asked me to be in the wedding, and then he said he would take Jude out tonight so that I could have a break. I nearly had a heart attack."

Luke's eyes bulged. "No way! Man, people can surprise you, huh?"

"Yeah, tell me about it. Well, I think I'll go lie down on my bed and do nothing," I said. "Enjoy a night to myself."

"Are you still pissed at me?" Luke asked, as I turned to leave.

"I was never *pissed* at you," I lied. "Just jealous, I guess."

"I get it," he said. "I remember how I felt when all my friends got to go to college after high school."

Oh yeah, I thought. *I remember how I felt when all of my friends got to finish high school. What did he have to complain about?*

"So, we're cool, then?" he asked.

"Yeah, we're cool," I said, wanting to be done with the conversation. "I need you to do one thing for me, though."

"Name it."

"Tina's dragging her feet about applying to schools. I thought you could talk to her. She'll listen to a big shot like you."

"Some big shot," he said. "But, yeah, I can do that. Tina's cool. She could go places."

"*And* she's hot," I added, hoping Luke would start remembering all of the reasons he and Tina had been friends in high school.

"She always was," he replied, as he fumbled around on the couch, looking for the remote.

"Well, I'm gonna call it a night. See ya in the morning."

"See ya," he answered.

I turned and started walking back up the stairs. When I got to the landing, I could hear the din of the TV, which for Luke was as good as a sleeping pill. "Call Tina before you fall asleep!" I yelled down the stairs.

"I will, promise!" he called back.

I turned the fan on and lay down on my bed in my boxers and a thin T-shirt to try and stay cool. I didn't often have alone time and maybe that was a good thing. I found myself thinking about Stephen—missing him.

"Right here, my man, that's it," said Stephen, guiding the roots of the fig tree into the large hole he had dug. Jude stood watching as I struggled to lift the weight of the tree. It was heavier than it looked.

"Stop, stop, you're good, now just lower it in slowly."

That wasn't happening, so I dropped it into the hole and fell onto the grass in relief. "I need more exercise," I panted.

Stephen laughed. "Well, I can definitely give you more exercise if that's what you want," he said playfully.

"Shut up," I whispered. "Not around Jude."

"Relax, he's not listening," said Stephen. "All he cares about right now is his fig tree."

"Wonder why?" I asked. "He goes on and on about the damn thing."

Stephen lay down next to me on the grass and closed his eyes. "It's Jude," he replied, as if that was an explanation in itself. "God's little gardener."

What's wrong with me? I thought, as I came out of my daydream. All I had to do was drive to the Center and tell Stephen that I needed him and that I wanted him back. He would come. He said he would wait for me, but why was I keeping him waiting? Something was holding me back; stopping me from stealing the keys to Luke's car and driving to the Center that very second. I had never felt that taking care of Jude was a punishment, but did I actually think that the three of us could live together like a normal family? Well, we wouldn't be *normal*; nowhere close. The question was if my life with Stephen and my life with Jude could be reconciled. I didn't know how they could. Before my parents died, it had just been Stephen and me. Jude was always a huge part of my life but not my whole life, not like now, where just about every thought and action revolved around *his* needs, *his* happiness. Along the way I had forgotten about my own.

I turned off the lamp on my bedside table. The room felt cooler without it on. I wanted to close my eyes for a minute, not fall asleep, but that's exactly what happened. I knew that I would hear Jude coming in and would wake up. But he never did and so I just slept and slept and slept.

CHAPTER 21

I felt a pair of strong hands gripping my shoulders and shaking me. I opened my eyes as my head collided with my pillow. It was Luke. He stopped shaking me when he realized I was awake and I could finally focus on his face. A shiver shot up my spine. He looked as if he'd seen a ghost or something. I rubbed my eyes, still lying down. "What's going on?"

"It . . . it's Jude," he stammered. "He's in trouble. We have to go to the police station, *now*."

I shot up in bed, nearly head-butting Luke. "What do you mean, trouble?"

Panic was setting in on Luke's face. "Man, I don't get it." His voice shook like he was about to cry. "Paul just called. He said Baptiste saw Jude wandering around the strip mall in the middle of the night and called the cops. They came and picked him up and . . ." He stopped mid-sentence.

"And what?" I demanded. He just stared at me like a dummy. "Luke! And *what*?"

He took a deep breath and found his voice again. "And when they picked him up, they found cocaine in his pocket. A *lot* of cocaine."

I started shaking my head. *No,* I thought. *This is the most twisted, sick joke I'd ever heard. I would go downstairs and find Jude sitting at the kitchen table drinking his orange juice and eating a waffle. This wasn't real. Maybe I was still dreaming.*

Luke jumped off the bed and began ripping open every drawer. When he didn't find what he was looking for, he started throwing stuff out of the closet. If I was still dreaming, this was a very vivid dream. He looked at me furiously. "Where is it?" he spat. "Simon, what have you been *doing*?"

Then it registered. This *was* real; very, very real. Jude was in jail, and Luke thought I was the reason he was in there.

"Are you out of your fucking mind?" I hollered, as I flew out of bed. I grabbed the pair of shorts that I'd tossed on the floor last night. I zipped them up and jammed my feet into a pair of sandals. Luke was first to the bedroom door, and I followed him out. He grabbed his keys from the hallway table.

"We'll talk about this when we get to the station and find Paul," he grumbled.

I didn't say anything in my defense because I had none. I didn't even know exactly what had happened, but I knew I was responsible. I should have been with Jude last night and I wasn't.

We got into Luke's truck, and he shot out of the driveway, barely checking to see if there was any oncoming traffic. He lay down hard on the gas all the way to the police station.

I felt trapped inside the stifling truck. "Goddamnit!" I shouted. "I *never* should have trusted the Captain! Why did I let him take Jude without me? How could I have been so stupid?"

"Hey, stop it," Luke cut in, gripping the steering wheel with one hand and my shoulder with the other. "I'm sorry I freaked out back there, all right? I know you didn't have anything to do with this."

Nothing he said was registering. All I could think about was how much I wanted to kill Paul.

Luke sped past the strip mall and across the railway tracks. The police station was a dreary concrete building next to a 7-11 and Dan's Anytime Bail Bonds. We parked out front and got out of the truck. We ran toward the glass doors and entered a small foyer. The rest of the station, including a reception desk, was sectioned off from the entrance with bulletproof glass. A clock hung on the wall above where the glass ended. It was seventeen minutes after eight. Luke approached a pudgy woman sitting behind the desk.

"Good morning," he said politely. The lady looked up and smiled. Luke's good looks had a powerful effect on people, especially women. I was hoping the officer who arrested Jude was a lonely female cop. Then maybe we'd have a chance.

"My name is Luke Peters," he continued, "and this is my brother Simon. Our other brothers are already inside, Paul and Jude Peters. Paul called us and told us to come to the station right away and that he would be waiting in the chief's office."

"All right, dear," she said. "Let me call the chief. You said your name was Luke?" He nodded. "Okay, hon, just a minute." She turned in her swivel chair and picked up the phone.

My breathing was uneven and my heart was beating so fast, I thought I might have a heart attack. I felt nauseous and crouched down, lowering my head between my knees. The last time I was here was after the car accident. We had all met with Chief Guidry and a nice lady from Social Services, Alison Chauvin. I wondered if Alison was in with the chief. Even if she wasn't, someone would have called her by now and she'd be on her way.

Luke crouched down beside me and wrapped his arm around my shoulder. "Come on, Simon, pull yourself together."

I thought of Jude and how scared he must have been. Luke was right. If I couldn't be brave for myself, then at least I needed to be brave for Jude. I raised my head and looked around. The dizziness seemed to be gone. I took a few deep breaths and slowly stood up, holding onto the counter for support.

"Thanks," I said. "I'm fine now. I dunno what just happened."

"It's called a panic attack," Luke answered, already sounding like a doctor. "You'll be fine."

A door to the right of us opened and an officer stepped into the foyer who reminded me of one of the G.I. Joe figures I played with as a kid. The clerk who had been speaking with Luke appeared again and spoke through the opening in the glass. "Boys, this is Officer Daigle, and he's going to take you to see the chief."

"Thank you, ma'am," Luke replied.

Officer Daigle nodded at us and then turned. We followed him silently through a narrow hallway with several doors on either side, all of them closed. We entered a larger office where three other officers like Daigle were sitting at desks. At the opposite end was a door that had Chief Guidry's name on it. Officer Daigle knocked and waited for someone to open it. Chief Guidry appeared in the doorway, looking tired and much older than I remembered him. He smiled weakly at Daigle. "Thanks, son," he said. Daigle nodded, turned, and left without a word. He didn't even glance at us. I felt like a criminal.

"Luke, Simon," he said. "Come on in, boys."

The chief's office was exactly the same as when we'd last been there. He had a heavy wooden desk stained a dark cherry brown. His desk was just about the nicest thing in the entire station. There was a large window on one wall and a door that led to an interrogation room on the other, like the kind you see on TV shows with one-way-glass. The chief had given us a tour the day we came to meet with him and Alison after the accident. She was in the room too, sitting on the chief's leather desk chair.

"Hi, Simon. Hi, Luke," she said in her soft Cajun voice.

"Hi, Alison," we murmured.

I turned and saw Paul leaning on the wall by the window with his hands resting on his hips. He didn't have to look at me or say a single word. The rage erupted all on its own.

"WHAT HAVE YOU DONE?" I shouted, lunging at him. I could almost taste the satisfaction of wrapping my hands around his neck and squeezing the breath out of his lungs, but Luke was bigger and faster. His arms felt like tight chains around my waist as he launched me off the ground and then bodychecked me into the opposite wall. Luke stood there in front me like a shield, and I knew I wasn't going anywhere, so I just started yelling. "All that stuff about 'water under the bridge!' That was all bullshit, wasn't it? You were supposed to be watching him!"

"I was watching him!" he shouted back. "I brought him home from the arcade, and he went upstairs to go to bed. I stayed downstairs with Lydia for a while and then *we* went to bed. I thought he was sleeping!"

I pushed against Luke, but he wouldn't budge. "You're lying! You know Jude doesn't get ready for bed by himself. If he was home he would have woken me up! I slept the entire night, which means he never *came* home!"

"Boys, that's enough!" shouted the chief. "I need you both to *calm down*. Simon, you haven't even given me a chance to tell you what happened."

"Yeah, what *Paul* says happened."

"Simon," Luke hissed. "You are just making this a million times worse. Can you please just *stop?*"

"Fine," I muttered through clenched teeth. Luke pulled back a bit, and I was able to duck under his arm into freedom. I looked at the chief. "Where's Jude? I want to see him, *now.*"

"He's next door. You can see him in a minute when you're less . . . agitated." He had his hands out in front of him like he was prepared to fight me off.

"You'll just upset him in this condition," added Alison. I hated to admit that she was right.

"Okay, fine," I said. "But can someone *please* tell me what the Hell is going on here?"

Paul started up again, but the chief silenced him immediately. "Paul, let me," he said firmly. "You want to take a seat, Simon?"

I shook my head. "I'm fine." I could barely stand still, let alone sit.

"Where to begin?" The chief sighed. "Well, we received a 911 call shortly after midnight from Mr. Baptiste who owns the Pilot Café. He said there was a young man loitering in the parking lot of the closed Stop 'n Save. He couldn't tell us if he recognized the boy, but there had been some drug activity in that area so one of my officers went to look into it. He saw your brother stumbling around like he was lost, and at first the officer thought he was drunk or high. He followed standard procedures and asked him to lean up against the car so he could search him and, well, that's when he found the cocaine. Thirty-five grams of it, for Heaven's sake. Jude wouldn't answer any of the officer's questions, so he had no choice but to book Jude for possession of a narcotic with the intent to sell."

I couldn't keep quiet after that. "You don't actually think that *Jude* is selling drugs, do you?" I asked.

"I don't know, Simon. What am I supposed to think?"

"This is a load of bullshit!" I spat. "Jude isn't even physically capable of doing that. For one thing, he's mute, and for another, he wouldn't go wandering off and get involved with criminals. It's impossible!"

"I think you might be underestimating him," said the chief.

The chief was right, but I couldn't let him know what I knew, which was that Jude had wandered off before and that we had a drug dealer living next door and probably one in our own house. "No, I'm the only one who's ever given him *any* estimation," I pointed out. "I'm the only one who knows him, and I *know* that he didn't do this!"

"Simon, the evidence is there. You can't just ignore it," said Paul.

"I can if it was *planted!*" I was about ready to pounce on him again, but Luke had moved in front of me.

"Jude orchestrating this on his own is . . . well, pretty skeptical, Paul, you have to admit that," said the chief.

Finally, I thought. *The man is coming to his senses.*

"But there is what you said about the Rafferty boy," said Alison timidly.

The chief nodded. "Yes, there is that. Did you know that your neighbor, Stanley Rafferty, is being investigated for drug trafficking?" he asked all three of us.

I looked at Paul whose eyes shot down to the floor. Luke's mouth was hanging open. Typical Luke, he was completely clueless.

"No," I answered. I couldn't let on that I knew what Stan was involved in. That would just make things look bad.

"Well, he is. Pretty sloppy at it too, I might add. He's under surveillance, and once we catch him in the act, he's going away for a *long* time."

The pieces were starting to come together. I guess Stan wasn't as dumb as he looked. He must have known that they were on to him, and so he was laying low. That's why he needed Paul to sell the stuff for him. No one would ever suspect Mr. Perfect. Then I remembered the day Stan took Jude into his garage to pick out the tools and how he had approached me on the road about working with him. Was that Paul's idea? I had thought Paul would want to keep an eye on Jude and me to protect his image, but maybe that wasn't the whole story. Was turning his drug ring into a family business how he planned to make my money problems "go away"?

The chief's voice interrupted my thoughts. "Now, I know that you boys have done your best to take care of Jude and his . . . ah, his special needs, but you couldn't have watched him all the time. Isn't it possible that this Stan character might have spoken to him one day? Through the fence in your backyard, perhaps, and convinced him to, oh I don't know, go play a game?"

"That proves nothing," I said. "Only that we have bad taste in neighbors. Why would Stan want to get Jude involved anyways? What good would that do him?"

"Maybe he was smart enough to realize that someone like Jude could fly under the radar and never be suspected," replied the chief.

"Okay, fine," I said, "*maybe* that's what happened, but why are we standing around here guessing? Just ask him. Jude will tell you this is just a *huge* misunderstanding."

"A misunderstanding?" the chief said skeptically. "Do you know the street value of what we seized? *Thousands* of dollars. This is serious, Simon."

I couldn't look at the chief or at Paul. I knew Paul would never admit to my face that he was involved in Stan's dealing. I stared through the window at the parking lot of the 7-11 and what was turning into another blistering hot day. No one had to explain to me that this was serious. *Go figure,* I thought. *The one time Paul tries to "help us," we end up in a police station.*

"Besides, Simon, we've tried to ask him," the chief added. "We've been questioning him all morning. He won't say anything. Now, granted, none of us here knows how to sign but we gave him paper and a pen and asked him to write down what happened, and he refuses to do it."

"That's why we asked you to come," said Alison. "We're hoping he'll tell you."

"Of course he'll tell me," I said confidently. There was nothing Jude kept from me. "Let me see him." I flashed Paul a smug look. Jude would tell me everything. How Paul never brought him home last night. How he and Stan put the drugs in his pocket and dumped him off in the vacant strip mall to fend for himself with a bunch of junkies. Or, maybe they were showing him what to do and then ran like cowards when they heard the police sirens.

The chief walked over to the door and opened it for us. Silently, we entered a rectangular room that looked into the interrogation room. Jude was hunched over a metal table, his hands clenched together. He looked miserable, but I'd expected him to look worse; to be in near convulsions, rather than just swaying gently the way he did when he was waiting at the kitchen table for dinner. I couldn't see his entire face, but from what I *could* see, he appeared almost calm.

CHAPTER 22

"I'll stay here, Simon, and let you go in and talk to Jude for a minute," said the chief. "We'll be able to hear you from inside this room."

Not if I whisper, I thought to myself. I followed the chief inside the second room. There were no windows, just concrete gray walls. One of the boxed lights flickered constantly, and the ancient AC unit mounted on the wall hissed as it spat out what little air it could.

Jude did not look at us when we entered. The chief patted me on the back as if to say "good luck" and then walked back out again. He closed the door behind him. I wasted no time sitting down on one of the card table chairs next to Jude. I put my arm around his shoulders and drew him in close. When I spoke, I wanted only him to hear. Jude didn't even acknowledge that I was there. His eyes remained fixed on a single spot on the metal table. I assumed that he was mad at me for leaving him with Paul the night before, and I didn't blame him.

"Jude, I'm *sorry,*" I whispered. "I never should have left you alone with him." I shook him a little, trying to get a response, but he did nothing. I decided on a different approach. "I know what happened," I continued. "I know you never came home last night, which means Paul is responsible for this, but I need you to back up my story or they won't believe me." His hands remained entwined like a giant ball of fingers. "Jude, you've *got* to talk me or you'll be in a lot of trouble. We all will. Do you understand that? A *lot* of trouble. They'll take you away. Put you in a home somewhere." Even with the threats, Jude didn't budge. I suddenly became afraid. What if he didn't want to talk to me? Jude's fingers slowly unwound, and he raised his right hand, still looking down. I held my breath as I waited for the words to appear on the page. He lifted the pen and placed the tip on the piece of paper. I looked at him expectantly as he dragged it down, making his first mark. But my hope was short-lived.

YOU WILL BE FINE. He wrote with slow, precise strokes. I was confused and waited for a few seconds for him to keep writing, but instead he put down the pen and remained perfectly still.

"No!" I whispered fiercely. "This isn't about *me*, it's about *you*!" Finally, Jude turned his head to look at me. His eyes were peaceful; his mouth curled into a little smile. *What is he thinking?* I wondered. *How can he be so calm while I'm a complete wreck?* He turned his attention back to the paper and lifted the pen again. "Good," I coaxed him. "Just tell me what happened so we can go home."

With the same meticulous strokes as before, Jude began to write in large letters. Again, he wrote one short sentence and put down the pen. I AM WAITING, it said.

"Waiting?" I asked. "Waiting for what?" Now I was getting frustrated. Why wouldn't he talk to me? Jude

didn't answer my question. He just continued to stare at the strange words he had written. I threw back the flimsy card table chair and hovered over him. "Jude, this is serious!" I grasped his thin shoulders and was prepared to shake the truth out of him. He resisted about as much as a rag doll would. "You tell me everything!" I reminded him. "I know I haven't always been honest with you, but *you*, you have never lied to me!" From behind, something large and heavy struck my back. A familiar pair of strong arms wrapped like a gurney around my waist and once again I found myself in the air. "YOU CAN'T DO THIS TO ME!" I hollered at the top of my lungs as Luke carried me out of the room. I saw Jude's face for only a split second before Alison came in and stood in front of him. I saw tears in his eyes, and his lips were pressed tightly as if he were trying to stop himself from calling out to me. It was the closest I had ever seen Jude to talking, or at least wanting to talk, yet he didn't say a word.

Once we were inside the chief's office and I had stopped squirming, Luke set me down carefully, but rather than just letting me go, he took my shoulders and hugged me.

"I'm sorry, Simon," he choked. There was pain in his voice, and I knew that I had an ally in Luke. He loved Jude. Maybe not as much as I did or half as much as our mother had, but still it was love and the only weapon I had to fight this evil thing that was happening.

"Why won't he talk to me?" I moaned, even though I knew that Luke wouldn't have an answer. I heard someone, or maybe two people, entering the office, and then the door slammed.

"Luke!" Paul growled. "Take Simon home, he's hysterical!"

"No!" I shouted. "I am *not* leaving."

Luke pulled away from me to glare at Paul. "He's just upset," he spat. "I wouldn't expect *you* to understand."

Paul's hand was shaking with anger but he managed to raise a finger and point it at Luke. "The chief only asked you two to come because he thought you might be able to help. Where I stand, *he* is only making things worse!"

"Boys!" exclaimed the chief. "What is going on here? I have never seen you argue this much!"

"Jude's kind of a touchy subject in our house," I replied.

"So I see. Well, right now I need you to put your differences aside and do what is in Jude's best interests, do you understand? Or, I *will* send you and Luke home, Simon."

"Yes, sir," I heard Luke mumble.

"So what do we do now?" I asked the chief. "He won't talk to me either."

"Alison made some calls this morning and she thinks there might be another way to help Jude give us an answer. It's a technique called facilitated communication."

Now the chief was thinking. I knew all about facilitated communication. Mom had done tons of research on it as a possible method of communication for Jude after it became clear that he would never speak. She had described it to me when I was old enough to understand. At first it sounded like a miracle. She had heard stories of children who could write entire sentences with the help of facilitators who would sit next to them and support their elbow as they selected keys on a computer or letter board. But for every story of success, there was another denouncing FC as a hoax. Who could tell if the communication was coming from the child or the facilitator? Mom didn't pursue it any further after Jude took so quickly to sign language. I hadn't thought about FC in years and now it was our last chance. I couldn't bring myself to believe it was a hoax—not if it could save my brother.

"I'm familiar with it," I said.

"Then you know that experts are divided on the subject, whether it works or not?"

"Yes."

"Good. I just . . . I want you to be prepared for a possible disappointment, that's all."

I was more concerned about what would happen if it *did* work, and not in the way I wanted it to. I had seen a TV documentary on FC with Mom and a part of the program was about FC and the law. "Chief, you should know that any statements you get from Jude using facilitated communication probably won't stand up in court."

"Yes, Alison told me that too," he replied. "But I have no intention of taking this to court. I care about you boys and I feel a certain degree of responsibility for you since your parents are gone. I just want to make this right and do what is best for Jude."

"So if you're not going to charge him, then why are we still here?" Luke asked.

"It won't happen again," I added. "I *promise*."

The chief took a deep breath and leaned against his desk. He looked over at Paul. I didn't like where this was going. "I still need to find out as much as possible about what happened," the chief said. "What Jude's involved in is very serious, boys, and *how* he got involved is just as serious. It may be in . . . well, everyone's best interest if Jude were in a place where he could receive more specialized care. I've got the public's safety to think about as well, you know."

Every muscle in my body seized. "You don't think we can take care of him, do you?" I asked. It was almost a whisper. I said "we," but everyone in the room except the clueless Chief Guidry knew I had meant "I"—that *I* couldn't take care of him.

"You've done the best you could," he replied. "No one is blaming any of you for this."

"Who can perform this facilitated communication thing," asked Paul impatiently. "How long will it take?"

"Alison spoke with a Dr. Reid over the phone. Her practice is in New Orleans and she agreed to drive up this morning to help. We're very lucky she's willing to do this, boys."

"Is Alison still with Jude?" I asked.

"Yes, she's going to stay with him until Dr. Reid arrives. Shouldn't be long now."

Shouldn't be long now? I thought. *New Orleans is four hours south of here.* "So you knew Jude wouldn't talk to me?" I asked miserably. "If Alison called this doctor before I even got here."

"I couldn't be sure, Simon, and I didn't want to waste any time."

I walked to a wooden chair in front of the chief's desk and sank down. I bent over and cradled my head in my hands.

"You boys can wait here," said the chief. "Get

yourselves something to eat and try to be patient. I'll bring in the doctor as soon as she arrives."

"Thanks," Luke mumbled. I felt his arm on my shoulder.

"I need some air," Paul muttered. He crossed the office and followed the chief out.

"Simon?" said Luke.

I looked up at him. "What did Jude tell you?" he asked. "We saw him writing stuff before you freaked out."

"That's just it," I fumed. "He told me nothing. That's *why* I freaked out."

"Nothing? He must have told you something."

"No! Just that I would be okay and that he was waiting."

"Waiting? For what?"

"That's what *I* said!" I was practically screaming. "Now do you see why I went ape shit in there?"

"Well, maybe he's waiting for this doctor."

"If he even knows there is a doctor," I said. "Which I doubt."

"I dunno, I can't think on an empty stomach. You hungry?"

I had to think about that for a few seconds. "Starving," I decided.

Luke went out to get us Dr Peppers and Hubig's pies from the 7-11. He devoured a pie in two mouthfuls and then moved on to the next one. I could hear my stomach growling, but when I took a bite of the crust, it tasted like dust. I spat it into a trash can. I drank the soda in tiny sips, tasting nothing.

"Why are you so mad at Paul?" Luke asked. "You don't really think he's involved in this, do you?"

"You thought *I* was," I shot back.

He looked down guiltily and crushed his empty Dr Pepper can. "I told you I was sorry."

"Yeah, I know," I replied. "It's Stan. Paul's been selling his stuff to Perrucci's boys."

Luke's mouth dropped open wide enough for me to see some cherry pie filling stuck to one of his teeth. "You'd better be able to prove that," he said. He wasn't threatening me. He was just being honest. Who would believe something like that without evidence? Unfortunately, what I had witnessed the other night on Gibsland Street was the only evidence I had, and I wasn't exactly citizen of the year.

"I saw a deal going down one night after work," I explained. "By the exact parking lot where they found Jude. The guy who Stan was selling to worked for Perrucci. I heard Stan say there was someone at the company who this guy could buy from in the future. There's no other explanation. Not with the amount of time that Paul's been hangin' around Stan."

"Well, if you're so sure, then why didn't you tell the chief?" he asked.

"Because *Jude* needs to tell the chief. He won't believe it coming from me. I have no real evidence. Besides, there's more. Stan came up to me yesterday and was trying to get *me* involved too."

"Well we definitely can't tell the chief *that*," he said. "It just proves his theory. If Stan was trying to rope you in, who's to say he didn't get to Jude first?"

"Yeah, I already thought of that. But I think *Paul* put Stan up to it. Paul either wanted me and Jude involved so we could make money and not be his problem anymore or he figured he could use the drug thing to blackmail us into doing whatever *he* might want." Paul had blackmailed me before, so I knew it wasn't beneath him. Apparently nothing was. "When Stan came up to me in the street, he said something about not wanting me to be a liability. If I'm a liability, then so is Jude."

"Sweet Jesus," Luke whispered. "What the Hell is going on here?"

"I dunno for sure."

"And the only person who does isn't talking," he said. *"Great."*

Luke was right. Doctor or no doctor, Jude was the only person who could get himself out of this mess. So why was he doing nothing? He hadn't regressed. He'd communicated with me in the interrogation room. *You will be okay. I am waiting.* What did that mean? At this rate he wasn't going to have to wait much longer before they shipped him off to some group home.

I began to think about what our lives would be like without Jude; what would happen if they took him away. It came to me then—the horrible truth that had been staring me in the face the entire time. He wasn't interested in protecting himself. Jude might have agreed to go with Paul and Stan not knowing it would bring him here, to this moment, but now that he was in it, he was going to give us what he thought we needed. *Him gone.*

CHAPTER 23

I sat in the chief's office thinking about everything I could have possibly done wrong. I analyzed everything I could remember ever saying to Jude or doing with him. Had I not protected him enough from Paul? Had Luke not watched him closely enough while I was at work? Jude had his moods but overall he seemed happy. We didn't have a lot, but I made sure he had everything important—food, clothes, *love*. Had I not loved him enough?

"I need to get outta here," I announced. Luke said nothing as I rushed to the door. Head down, I passed the officers and the lady behind the bulletproof glass. The sun was beating down hard on the parking lot, so I hung back under the overhang where there was a soda machine and a bench. The questions began streaming through my mind like news flashes. How could he just leave me? After everything we've been through? *You will be okay?* How? Everything was falling apart.

I slumped down onto the bench. I sat there mindlessly watching the cars drift back and forth and listening to the soft crunch of the pavement under their tires. I don't know how long I sat there.

"Simon." I looked up. It was the chief. "The doctor called. She'll be pulling in any minute now. Why don't you come back inside?"

I slowly stood up and followed him, still in a daze. Inside the chief's office, Luke hadn't budged. I resumed my place by the window and kept my eyes on the ground, not saying anything. We waited in silence for a few minutes until the chief walked into his office, followed by Paul and a plain-looking woman dressed in a brown business suit. Dr. Reid had a kind smile and I decided Jude would feel comfortable around her. She introduced herself to Paul and Luke and then walked toward me.

"You must be Simon," she said.

I nodded. "Thanks for coming."

"I just hope that I can help," she replied. "I understand that you're Jude's primary caregiver."

"Yes, and I want to be there when you talk to him," I blurted out.

Paul tried to protest, but Dr. Reid cut him off. "Of course," she said. "Jude should have people around him whom he trusts."

"We're all going," said the chief. "This way, Dr. Reid." He opened the door to the interrogation area. I stayed close to the doctor, afraid that the chief would shut the door before I could get inside. Luke and Paul dragged their feet behind us. Once inside, the chief handed Dr. Reid a piece of paper.

"The questions, Doctor. There are three to get started," he explained. Dr. Reid scanned the sheet and nodded. She slid the page into the front pocket of her canvas briefcase.

Alison was sitting next to Jude with her arm around

him. My heart sank. He just sat there miserably, still and quiet. He was waiting, but not for any kind of redemption. He was waiting for this doctor and the final judgment.

Alison got up to introduce herself to the doctor and then turned back to Jude, touching his shoulder. "Jude, this is Dr. Reid. She's come to sit with you for a few min- utes." Jude nodded slightly but didn't look up.

Dr. Reid never let her smile fade for a second. "It's nice to meet you, Jude," she said. "May I set up my things next to you?" Again Jude nodded. The doctor placed her brief-case on the table. For a second she looked up at me and the smile was gone. It seemed that, like me, she knew there was something going on that didn't feel right. The doctor turned her bright smiley face back on as she opened up a small laptop computer. "Do you like computers, Jude?" she asked. Jude shrugged.

"He won't use our home computer," I said. "He doesn't like the bright light, but I don't think it scares him or anything."

"Oh, well, using a computer is very simple, Jude," she continued. "I am going to type a question at the top of a blank page, and I will gently hold your arm for support. I need you to type out an answer to the question, with either a yes or a no. Can you do that for me?" Again Jude nodded just slightly. Dr. Reid pulled up a Word document and started typing. When she was finished, she placed the computer in front of Jude and sat down next to him on his right hand side. She asked Jude to show her where the Y on the keyboard was and then the E. They reviewed the location of all the letters needed to spell the words yes and no. I went to stand behind Jude so that I could see what answers he was typing. "Are you ready?" she asked. Jude raised his eyes to look at the bright computer screen.

Dr. Reid placed one hand gently on his right shoulder and with the other she took Jude by the elbow and guided his hand over the keyboard. At this point, Jude was supposed to spell out his answer without any assistance from Dr. Reid. This was where all of the controversy about FC came from, but that wasn't what I was concerned about. I had no doubt that Jude was going to answer on his own and that Dr. Reid might as well not even be in the room. I stood there holding my breath, feeling completely helpless. It was up to Jude now.

"Jude, the question is: Do you understand that you were found with thirty-five grams of cocaine in your pocket on the morning of July twenty-sixth at twelve-thirty-six AM?"

Jude's eyes looked down at the keys. He raised his index finger and made three distinct motions. Y, then E, then S.

I took a breath, afraid that if I didn't I would pass out on the floor. *Don't panic,* I thought. *Of course he answered yes. He's not stupid. He knows he was caught with it. The question is how it got there.*

"Thank you, Jude," said Dr. Reid. She released Jude's elbow and let his arm rest on his lap. She saved the first page and then opened another blank document where she typed the second question. Turning the computer back toward Jude, she repeated the same procedure and brought Jude's right arm back into the typing position.

"Jude, the question is: Did you bring the cocaine to the parking lot with the intention of selling it to someone?"

Jude did not hesitate. His hand robotically spelled YES. Dr. Reid read aloud Jude's answer. There was no smugness on Paul's face, just a look of peacefulness. He knew that his gold coins would be waiting for him outside in his new life without Jude. Dr. Reid looked up at the chief, not quite sure what to do next.

"Ask him the last question," I demanded. My voice sounded strange, like it wasn't my own. My whole body seemed detached from my mind. I stood perfectly still, not sure if I could move even if I wanted to.

Dr. Reid again saved the document and opened a new page. She typed quickly; the clicks of the keys sounding like a judge's gavel pounding in my ears. "Jude, the next question is: Did you go to the parking lot on the night of July twenty-fifth with the intention of selling the cocaine on your own accord, having not been forced by anyone to do so?"

This was Jude's chance to reveal what had really happened and who was actually responsible, but the way Paul leaned against the wall like nothing could touch him made me worried. For a third time Paul refused to come to Jude's defense, but then again, neither did I. Was I a coward for saying nothing or, if I loved my brother, was it time to let him choose?

With Dr. Reid's arm propped up under his elbow, Jude lifted his finger and pressed the first key, then the second, and then the third. Three letters that changed our lives forever. YES.

Jude pulled his arm away from Dr. Reid and clasped his hands tightly in between his knees. He bowed his head like a little kid who had just been put in time out. I lifted one hand onto his shoulder, but he did not turn around.

I looked up at the chief. Even though he had not been as confident of Jude's innocence as I had expected, he seemed shocked to actually have proof of his guilt. "Alison," the chief said. "Would you escort Dr. Reid back to my office, please? I'll just be a minute."

Dr. Reid closed her laptop and rose quietly from her seat. For a moment our eyes met, and I could see that she was truly sorry that this had happened. I don't think she believed his answers either, but as a supporter of FC she had to accept that they were the answers he had meant to give. Dr. Reid picked up her briefcase and followed Alison out of the room.

"Jude," said the chief firmly. "I am going to give you one more chance. Is there *anything* else you want to tell us about what happened last night? Anything at all?"

Jude raised his hands. "There is nothing more to tell," he signed. He lowered one hand back onto his lap, and he placed the other on top of mine. The chief shook his head.

"What now?" whispered Luke.

The chief inhaled deeply. "Well, Jude has just confessed to a class A felony." I started to protest when he interrupted me. "Yes, yes, I know, Simon. This confession may get thrown out of court but it also might not, which is why Alison and I need to clean this up as soon as possible. No one was harmed and the drugs never passed hands so we are going to just make this whole thing go away."

"How do we do that?" Luke asked.

"Alison thinks that the best thing is for Jude to spend some time in a specialized care group home. Jude would live with three or four other people his age under more careful supervision than what he's used to now. Some homes are specifically for nonverbal individuals like Jude, and according to Alison, the closest home with an opening is in Oklahoma."

"Oklahoma!" I shouted.

"It's closer than you think," said Paul.

I shot him a wicked glare. Of course, Oklahoma was much too close for the Captain's taste. He would have preferred Alaska.

"Can he come home with us until he has to leave?" I asked miserably.

The chief shook his head. "Again, Alison thinks it would be best if he stayed in a state-operated facility. She wants to make sure he stays out of trouble."

"And what do you think?" I asked, hoping our friendship with the chief might convince him to change his mind.

He looked at Jude and then at me. "I don't know exactly what's going on here," he said. "But what I do know is that I can't help a boy who won't help himself."

My shoulders slumped under the weight of his decision, knowing that it was final. "Y'all can visit him, of course," he added as he walked toward the door. "Alison and I will be talking later today with Paul about the details, so Paul can pass them on to the rest of you. But in the meantime, I'll . . . ah, I'll give you boys a few minutes." The chief shook his head, not quite sure what to make of us, and left the room.

The latch on the door had barely clicked closed when Luke raced over to where Jude was sitting and hoisted him out of his seat into a tight hug. "It'll be okay, little buddy, it'll be okay," he kept repeating over and over, but it was only himself he was trying to convince. He let go of Jude and stared in disbelief as Paul marched toward the door. "And where are you going?" Luke demanded.

"Where am I going? Where do you think I'm going?" he shouted. "I'm gonna go do what I've been doing for the last year! I'm gonna go be the adult here and fix another mess! I know what y'all think of me right now, but I have *always* done what was in the best interests of this family, and you know what else? My family doesn't just include the three of you anymore." With everything that had been going on, I had completely forgotten about Lydia and the baby. "I have a fiancée and a child to think about now and you three . . . you're just gonna have to grow up."

The door swung open, and he disappeared into the next room. Normally, I would have agonized over Paul's disapproving words, but not then. They didn't matter half as much as the person standing in front of me: Jude, my twin, who had been my conscience and everything else that was good in me. I wrapped my arms around him. I had taken him for granted, having never thought that I could lose him and certainly not in this way. "Are you sure you want to do this?" I whispered. He reached up and held my arm, which was as good as any answer. He was certain, but not only that, he wasn't afraid.

CHAPTER 24

It was the hardest thing I have ever had to do. Packing our room; putting Jude's things in one set of boxes and mine in another; knowing that they were going to two very different places. Luke paced back and forth, occasionally picking something up and putting it into a box. He was too upset to be all that helpful.

Luke sat down on the corner of Jude's bed. "Simon, I gotta tell you something," he said.

"Go ahead." I felt numb and so I figured this was the best time for Luke to drop whatever bomb he had coming.

"I'm moving to Baton Rouge at the end of the week. I got a place lined up with an old friend from high school." He looked down guiltily, but I was already over it.

"That's good," I replied and kept packing.

Luke stared at me, not sure what to make of my response. "Simon, you gotta understand," he moaned. "I *have* to get out of here."

"I do get it, Luke," I said, almost laughing. Though I'm not really sure why I found it funny. "I'm not mad. Go, there's nothing for you here anyways."

"You're here," he replied.

I was holding Jude's brown Cub Scout uniform that had been shoved into the back of a drawer. I ran my finger over the rough patches Mom had sewn along the arm. "Not for long," I whispered.

Luke didn't say anything, he just nodded. He probably knew better than to ask me what I was going to do. I simply didn't know. All I knew was that doing nothing wasn't an option anymore.

I found Jude's scrapbook the day he left for the home. I flipped through the pages of poems and stick-figure drawings. I worried about his garden and especially the fig tree. Paul and Lydia had decided to sell the house and get their own place. "Starting over," Paul called it. I doubted anyone would be able to keep the garden looking the way Jude had. No one would have the patience to carefully pull out each weed from the roots so it wouldn't grow back. No one would want to give up the comfort of the fans and go outside in the summer heat to water the flowers. Jude and the garden; I didn't know what the future held for either of them.

When I came to Stephen's page, I stopped and let my mind wander.

"Come on, Jude!" I called. "You can do it!" I was treading water in the lake by the Lévesques' cottage, pleading with Jude to jump off the high rock instead of the lower one, something he had never had the courage to do.

"Come on, please! Do it for me?" He was shaking his head and creeping further and further away from the ledge.

Stephen swam over to me. "Jude!" he shouted. Jude peered down at him. "You're the White Ranger and you must cross Lord Zedd's force field in order to retrieve the stolen Zeo Crystal. But only the brave can pass through!"

I gawked at Stephen, surprised he'd paid that much attention to Jude's Power Rangers obsession. By the time I looked up again, Jude was no longer on the cliff. He was catapulting through the air, his arms flailing and his mouth wide open, though clearly grinning. Stephen and I both laughed. Even when flying, Jude never made a sound.

I ran my fingers over the page. Stephen was always kind to Jude, but in the year he'd been gone, Jude had come to depend on me more than ever. I might not have seen it happening, but Jude must have.

I flipped through the rest of the scrapbook. There were dozens of empty pages in the book that he hadn't gotten the chance to do anything with. The last page he had started had his own name written in large, capital letters at the top, but the rest of it was blank. I had been holding it together pretty well until that moment; until I saw the empty page that I should have helped fill and now wouldn't get the chance to. I shut my eyelids tightly like a dam against the tears falling onto the lifeless page. I immediately closed the scrapbook and packed it in Jude's suitcase with his box of colored pencils.

Tina came with Luke and me to see Jude off. It didn't feel real, which made it a little bit easier to accept. I wandered through that day in a haze of denial. Jude never doubted his decision. In fact, he seemed more certain about it than he had about anything else in his life, even more certain than the day he told me he was going to plant a fig tree in our jungle of a backyard.

We pulled into the parking lot of the police station

where Chief Guidry was standing next to a white sedan, which had to be Alison's. She had called the house the day after Jude confessed to everything with the address and number of the group home he would be living in. As she'd expected, the home was in Tulsa, Oklahoma.

Luke pulled up next to them. In a useless protest, Luke and I refused to take any of Jude's stuff out of the trunk, so the chief finally began moving everything over to Alison's car. He didn't complain though. He looked as if he understood.

Luke and then Tina hugged Jude good-bye. I stood there staring at Jude, not sure if it was him, or me, who I no longer recognized. I grabbed him and held on as tight as I could.

"I'll call you," I choked, unable to say anything else. I could hear Tina crying behind me.

After a little while Jude pulled away from me. He looked so calm. "We'll see each other again soon," he signed.

Alison pushed open the passenger door from inside the car. Jude dropped into the seat and rolled down the window. He waved to us with a grin on his face as the white sedan drove away. I stood there for a few minutes, staring at the spot that had been the window. After a while, Tina reached for my hand.

"Come on," she said. "We need to go."

I took that as we needed to move on. That I couldn't stand on the curb thinking about how life would be different if I could do it all over again. What would be the point? My regret wasn't why Jude had given up everything. He wanted to give me a gift I couldn't give myself, and that was Stephen, the freedom to be with him. I couldn't thank him, not enough anyways, for what he had done for me, and for Stephen. But he hadn't done it for my thanks, either. Maybe he had done it out of love; to show me what it meant to be a real brother. Or maybe like so many things Jude did or said, I was just never meant to understand.

Living in the house without Jude seemed like unnecessary punishment, so I had decided I would move out that afternoon. I took Tobey up on his offer to let me crash at his place until I figured things out. Tina's Sunfire sputtered into the driveway around three in the afternoon like it was about to die. I was sitting on the front steps of our house with my entire life's possessions in boxes behind me on the porch. Kind of sad, really. It wasn't a very big porch.

"Let's just hope my car doesn't break down and make us have to carry all this stuff through that sketch neighborhood," muttered Tina.

We loaded up the trunk and the backseat with the boxes, shoving my pillows and sheets into whatever cracks we could find. I guided Tina out of the driveway, because she couldn't see a thing through the back window.

Tina was unusually quiet on the drive across town. She had the radio turned up really high so talking wasn't an option. I sat next to her in the passenger seat with a small duffel bag on my lap and some grocery bags full of books and shoes by my feet. We drove past the strip mall, and I took a good look at the Stop 'n Save for the first time since I'd been fired. The parking lot was jammed, and people were streaming in and out, completely oblivious to what actually went on inside those concrete walls. Not surprisingly, the Pilot Café was as dead as the Stop 'n Save was busy. At first I could have killed Baptiste for calling the cops on Jude. He phoned the house not long after we'd all gotten back from the station and spoke to Luke. I listened in from the hallway.

"How could you have known it was him?" Luke asked. There was a pause while Baptiste talked.

"But for all you knew, he could have been a psychopath with a gun," reasoned Luke. "Going out to check wouldn't have been smart." Luke then explained to him what was going to happen to Jude. There was another brief pause. "I dunno know why either," he replied miserably. "You're right, he hasn't done anything wrong."

It was obvious Baptiste was sorry or he wouldn't have called, and the more I blamed him the worse I felt. What happened back in that interrogation room was what Jude had decided needed to happen. He knew that if he took the blame he'd be shipped away like Stephen and that I'd move on with my life without him. Whether I wanted to or not. Blaming Baptiste wasn't going to change that fact.

Tina reached over to the dial and turned down the radio. "I talked to Luke," she said. There was some hesitation in her voice, and she purposely kept her eyes focused on the road.

"Oh yeah? You two make big plans?"

Tina shrugged. "Nothing crazy, you know. He's just gonna make sure I have everything I need to apply for the spring semester, stuff like that."

Perfect, I thought. *But I guess it's no surprise Luke came through on a favor that involves a good-looking single girl.*

"That's a start," I said. "But what are you gonna do until January around *here*?"

We drove for a while in silence as she tried to figure out the best way to tell me whatever it was she was afraid to tell me. But I wasn't afraid. I had a feeling I already knew. Tina and Luke would be good together, and really, all she needed to care about was that he was her ticket to college and to a better life. Helping out Tina was the least Luke could do after bailing on me.

"Well that's the thing," she began. "Your brother's renting a house with someone he knew from high school who's in Hospitality at LSU. He said you might remember him. Rob Hebert? But the place is a three bedroom so he asked me, you know, if I might be interested in moving in now since I need a place to live and a new job anyways.

I let out a chuckle, and the look of confusion on her face was priceless. "What's so funny?" she asked.

I smiled and then started singing: "Luke and Tina sittin' in a tree. K-I-S-S-I-N-G . . ."

"Oh stop!" she squealed, punching me as hard as she could in the shoulder.

"Who knows," I went on. "I might drive to Baton Rouge one day and find out I have a sister-in-law."

"Oh whatever!" she whined, but I could tell she was enjoying it. "So you're not mad then?" she asked.

No, I thought, *I'm done with being mad, but I can't help being a little envious.* Not of Tina, exactly, but of the life she had waiting for her. All of the pieces of her future had come neatly together, and I couldn't even find the pieces of my own. "No," I answered and quickly changed the subject. "Luke told me he had a place, but didn't say it was with Rob. He's pretty cool. You'll get along fine."

"You should think about my idea to come with us," she said. "You told me you couldn't because Luke needed a break from Jude, but, well, Jude's gone now."

I waited a few seconds before answering so that she would think I was at least considering the offer. It was nice and all, just not an option. "Thanks," I said with a little smile, "but four's a crowd. Y'all need to do your own thing." I stared out the window as we blurred past a gas station and roadside tomato stand. "Besides, I've got some loose ends to tie up here."

I had been at Tobey's apartment for a few days when the reality finally set in. I was jobless, homeless, and essentially family-less. Jude and Luke were gone and the Captain, well, he may have been blood, but he was no closer to being family than Stan or Jeb.

"You're not homeless," Tobey kept insisting. "I told ya, you can stay here as long as you need to."

I knew that Tobey meant it, and the good news was that he was going to get a job and be fine. They'd announced that the new Home Depot would open early next year. He knew nothing about tools, but as he put it, "I can put 'em in bags and tell people how much they cost."

Tobey started reminiscing about our shifts at the Stop 'n Save like they were the "good old days." I couldn't help but wonder for a second if maybe they were. I shook the thought, not wanting it to take hold, and excused myself. I went to the landing and puffed on an Ultra Light cigarette, thinking about my "loose end." The Lévesques,

Paul, and our entire church, had tried everything possible to break Stephen and me apart. And I'd almost let them. After all that Stephen and I had been through, would that love be enough to hold us together now? I couldn't know for sure, but I was more afraid of *not* trying and insulting Jude's sacrifice by letting Stephen rot away in that prison. They both deserved better than that, and so did I. There'd be no sneaking around this time either. I was going to walk through the front doors of the Waverley Christian Center with dignity and demand to see Stephen. He wouldn't doubt my feelings for him then.

I stepped on the lingering cigarette and went back inside to ask Tobey if I could borrow his car keys.

"I'll drop the car back to you as soon as I pick up Stephen," I said. "Then I'll be out of your way."

"But where y'all gonna go?" Tobey asked.

"I dunno yet," I replied. "But wherever it is, it'll have to be by bus."

"Well, at least let me drive you guys to the bus station."

"Thanks, man," I said. "I owe you big time. I'll see ya later."

"Do you want me to come with you?" he asked, just before I closed the door behind me.

"Nah, it's okay. I think I need to go this one alone." I smiled at him so he'd know I was going to be all right.

I seized the railing and launched down the stairs, taking three or four steps at a time. I jogged to Tobey's car: a black four-door sedan with more than enough scratches and dents to show its age. I unlocked the door and dropped down into the tan seat, which was raging hot from the sun. I turned on the car and cranked the AC to high. As the jets of cool air poured over my hands and face, I took a deep breath and shifted the gear into reverse.

I actually *did* want Tobey to come with me, but at the same time, I didn't know how to show my feelings for Stephen in front of anyone. Not even Tina. It still felt forbidden and the moment Stephen sat next to me in Tobey's car, we'd be fugitives running from a law that would condemn us no matter how far away we drove. There would always be people who'd think we were wrong for loving each other, but I knew that I could stop believing they were right. I'd just have to accept that for now, it was only my own mind I could change.

On the highway, I rested my arm on the windowsill, letting the breeze brush past my hand. I smiled, remembering how when we were small, Jude would practically climb out of the car window to feel the air streaming across his face. I knew, no matter how far away he was, Jude was still rushing at life with his eyes closed and his mouth open, feeling everything and loving everyone. This wasn't the end. Not for Stephen, not for me, and certainly not for Jude. This was only just the beginning.